DAWN WITH

Never Say Duke
Dukes, Actually
The Duke's Bride
The Duke's Embrace
The Duke's Desire
Dawn With a Duke
One Night With a Duke
Ten Days With a Duke
Forever Your Duke

*Gothic Love Stories*:
Too Wicked to Kiss
Too Sinful to Deny
Too Tempting to Resist
Too Wanton to Wed
Too Brazen to Bite

*Magic & Mayhem*:
Kissed by Magic
Must Love Magic
Smitten by Magic

CRESSMOUTH GAZETTE

**Welcome to Christmas!**

Our picturesque village is nestled around Marlowe Castle, high atop the gorgeous mountain we call home. Cressmouth is best known for our year-round Yuletide cheer. Here, we're family.

The legend of our twelve dukes? Absolutely true! But perhaps not always in the way one might expect...

～

# CHAPTER 1

*December 1814*

lthough Lady Isabelle Borland's carriage climbed toward the northernmost peak of England, she did not gaze out of the window in her usual dreamy way at the picturesque snow-blanketed landscape shimmering in all directions.

Instead, all of Belle's worried focus centered on the lady's maid seated opposite her.

Ursula's perpetually cheery freckled face was white as plaster of Paris, and drawn into a pained grimace that worsened every time one of their wheels ran over a rock or slid on a patch of ice. Her painstakingly styled russet hair clung to her face and neck in damp hunks, partially obscuring the rivulets of sweat dripping from her temples. Her shaking limbs hid beneath every single blanket in the carriage, save for a pale, trembling hand that clutched a sturdy sack that had once contained periodicals for the journey, and now contained...

Ah, there she went again. It had been ages since Ursula last attempted to eat, yet her stomach continued to rebel with alarming regularity.

"How much longer?" Belle shouted to their driver, John.

A lady did not shout, particularly not if she were the infallibly respectable daughter of a duke, but if Ursula did not get out of this carriage and into a warm bed posthaste—

"Two hours," John called back.

Two *hours?* Ursula would not last two more hours. The putrid sack swinging ominously from her fingers would withstand even less. And if Belle was sitting in the enclosed carriage when the contents of that sack escaped, John would deal with not one but two violently ill passengers.

"You have half an hour," Belle shouted back. "Maybe less."

"Lady Isabelle, I'm afraid horses cannot fly. Cressmouth is at the top of this mountain, and we must wind our way up the path like we do every year. With the way this snow is coming down—"

"Forget Cressmouth," Belle snapped. "I don't care about my holiday. Ursula needs a bed and a doctor."

John gestured at the endless horizon of rolling, snow-dusted pines and muttered what sounded suspiciously like, "Let me know when you see one."

She curled her fingers into fists. John couldn't

make horses fly, and Belle couldn't conjure a doctor out of thin air. But she had to do *something*.

*Think*, she begged herself in desperation.

*Females don't have to think*, Papa liked to say, with an indulgent wink. *That's what husbands and fathers are for. Just be pretty.*

And Belle would grit her teeth behind a tight-lipped smile to keep the frustration from boiling over as her mother's face fell with disappointment. *Lady Isabelle, were you thinking again? How will you ever find a match that way? There are rules to follow, darling. You know them by heart. All you need to do is follow them.*

Father was gone now, but the rules had not changed. All of Society followed them. What to say, what to do, what to eat, what to wear. What was allowed to interest you, who you could and could not befriend.

Like Ursula, for instance. Belle had been scolded time and again that Ursula was a *servant*, not a playmate. After more than a decade of each other's company, Ursula was no longer Belle's secret friend, but more like a sister.

And that sister was turning inside out in misery before Belle's eyes.

"Houville," she blurted.

John glanced back at her. "What?"

"Houville," she repeated in triumph. "It's the last little village before the long stretch to Cressmouth, and I don't recall having passed it."

John brightened. "You're right. I don't know if there'll be a doctor, but I believe there's a posting house. Can you last half an hour?"

Ursula gave Belle a weak nod before returning her face to her sack.

*Twenty minutes will be too long*, Belle wanted to respond, but did not. With all this ice and snow, a carriage accident would make things immeasurably worse.

"Thank you, John," she called back, and straightened the blankets about Ursula's shoulders.

Her brother, the Duke of Nottingvale, held a Yuletide party at his winter residence in Cressmouth every winter. Belle had thought it would be lovely to head up early and spend a week or two with her friend Angelica. She'd thought Ursula would enjoy the trip as well. She'd thought it might be a welcome holiday for them both.

And now this.

This was what she got for *thinking*.

She diverted her gaze out of the window to the passing evergreens. Each tree brought them closer to Houville. Everything would be fine. They would rent the finest suite of rooms in the posting house, Ursula would improve quickly, and they'd be back on the road to Cressmouth as if nothing had happened.

There wouldn't even be a need to mention this small detour to anyone. Especially not to her mother or to her brother, the duke.

It was all under control.

Or would be, as soon as they arrived at the posting house.

The moment evergreens turned into cottages with snow-covered roofs and busy brick chimneys, Belle tied her bonnet beneath her chin and set about helping Ursula prepare to leave the coach.

Snowflakes whirled in with the sharp wind as John swung open the carriage door.

She hurried down the step and onto the frozen street. "Don't worry about the trunks. We need to get Ursula inside. If you can take her, I'll run ahead and arrange the rooms."

"As you wish." John disappeared into the carriage.

Belle squinted up at the illustrated owl on the sign above the posting house door. *The Hoot & Holly*. At least it was open.

The interior teemed with people and warmth. Glasses and cutlery clanged in a crowded dining area that seemed to take up the front half of the building. At the rear was a long bar, behind which stood an older woman in an apron and a mob cap.

A lady did not rush, but time was of the essence. Belle hastened through the dining area, dodging wooden chairs and a harried serving girl.

When she reached the bar, the older woman flung a damp towel over her shoulder. "How can I help you, love?"

"I need three rooms for the night. And a doctor, if you've got one."

"I haven't." The woman passed a speculative glance over Belle's luxurious but hopelessly wrinkled traveling costume. "What's wrong with you?"

"Not me," Belle explained. "It's my maid. She's feverish, and cannot keep anything in her stomach. I'll take the finest suite you have, with separate bedrooms of course, and another room for our driver. We'll be on our way to Cressmouth as soon as—"

"Haven't got three rooms." The older woman pointed out of the window to the falling snow. "Suddenly everyone wants to stop here on their way to the castle. Too bad no one's a carpenter to add on another floor."

"What *do* you have?" Belle asked desperately. "I'll pay double."

The proprietress tilted her head and gave her a speculative look. "I've only one room left."

"Perfect." Belle sagged with relief. "I'll take it."

"It has but one bed," the proprietress warned. "A narrow one."

"My maid can have it," Belle said quickly. "I'll sleep on a chair."

Or on the floor. She'd brought enough gowns to improvise a cushion fit for a princess, if need be. But what was she to do with John?

Movement rustled behind her as her driver staggered forth with Ursula in his arms, the sack dangling from one pale hand.

The proprietress's eyes filled with compassion. "Caught the influenza that's going around, did she?"

John and Belle exchanged startled looks.

"Going around?" he croaked.

"It doesn't matter," Belle said firmly. "I'll mind her in my room." She turned to the proprietress. "Have you anywhere my driver could sleep?"

"I suppose you don't mind servants' quarters?"

John shook his head. "Not at all, madam."

6

"Then there's a bed for you." She narrowed her eyes at Ursula. "And for this one, as well. None of this 'sleeping on the floor' in my inn, when I've already a sickroom in the back for a maid who came down with the same thing. It'll be easier on everyone to keep the invalids in one place."

"Thank you." Belle pressed her hands to her heart. "You've no idea how much I appreciate your kindness."

"You may change your mind. The room I mentioned is the smallest one in the posting house. We try to keep men and women on separate floors, but with this weather, we're all having to make do. I suppose you have a companion?"

Belle's companion was barely conscious, and about to be carried off to the servants' quarters by her driver. Her skin went clammy. The daughter of a duke could not possibly spend a single moment by herself on a mixed-sex wing of bedchambers, much less pass an entire night in such company and expect to keep her reputation intact.

But what choice did she have? Dragging Ursula back out into the snow at twilight would be asinine and dangerous.

"It's fine," she said firmly. She would have a sturdy footman guide her to her room and stay locked in there until morning, when she could ring for a maid to accompany her back down. "Just me, no companions."

The proprietress slid a guestbook across the counter. "Then sign here, Miss...?"

"La—" Belle's voice cut off. She could *not* sign

"Lady Isabelle" in the registry. The scandalous news would arrive back in London before she did.

She needed a pseudonym. One that apparently began with "Lay," now that she'd begun.

"Lépine," she blurted. It had been the name of her childhood pet. It would have to do. "Mrs. Lépine. I'm... a widow. Traveling from... Epping."

Now she was babbling and giving far too much unnecessary information. She clamped her teeth shut before she invented three children and a chalet in France to match her fake French surname. If challenged, at least Belle could speak French. Those endless tutoring sessions had not been for nothing.

John, for his part, did not blink at the false name.

Nor did the proprietress, who tapped the pencil laying in the fold of the registry. "How do you do, Mrs. Lépine? I'm Mrs. Price. Sign, and I'll give you a key."

Belle grabbed the pencil and dashed an illegible scrawl on the next line. "Ursula and John are to have anything they wish. I will cover all costs. And if there's a doctor—"

"He'll be passing through tomorrow morning. I'll have him look at your girl when he attends the others. Now, shall we get the invalid out of our dining room?" Mrs. Price waved down an adolescent boy, and gave him instructions for both Ursula and John. Then she plucked a brass key from behind the counter and pressed it into Belle's hand. "There you are, love. Room eighteen. Third floor, second-to-last room on the left."

"Er..." Belle's fingers closed about the heavy key. "Is there someone who can carry up my trunks, and show John what to do with the carriage?"

Mrs. Price glanced about the busy dining room. "Not at the moment, but I'll see to it you're next. Why don't you have something to eat while you wait?"

"I'm not—" A rumble in her stomach made a lie of her protestation.

She *was* hungry, Belle realized. It had been hours since Ursula last ate, and the same amount of time for her. Belle had concentrated so hard on trying to arrive at Cressmouth before nightfall, for Ursula's sake, that she'd forgot all about stopping for food.

"I will," she told Mrs. Price. "Thank you. Please see that my driver eats as well."

Now that she'd woken her stomach, Belle realized she was famished. She turned in search of an empty table.

There was none.

"Always crowded this time of year." Mrs. Price beamed with pride. "We're the last posting house before Christmas."

Literally and figuratively. Cressmouth was best known as Christmas, and Britons flocked from far and wide to spend the festive season in a village renowned for its perennial Yuletide. Most revelers spent their holiday in beautiful Marlowe Castle, in one of hundreds of guest rooms with a spectacular view.

None of which was helping Belle find an

empty table. Perhaps over there... No. Or perhaps over... Taken, as well. Or perhaps—

A pair of glittering brown eyes met hers and Belle's breath caught in her suddenly dry throat.

The gentleman gazing back at her looked as though he had just stepped out of a fashionable gentleman's club such as White's or Brooks's. Gleaming black Hessians on his feet, flawless buckskins molded to his legs, an exquisitely tailored frock coat over an understated waistcoat. Dark hair, darker gaze. Neckcloth so bright it dazzled the eyes. Every stitch was perfect, every hair in place. He was like a portrait entitled *Dangerous Rake: Virtuous Ladies Should Not Dare Come Near.*

And he was beckoning her closer. No, not merely *closer.* He was gesturing to the empty seat on the other side of his private table. He was inviting her to join him.

Her heart clattered. She shouldn't. She *wouldn't.* It was improper in every way... for Lady Isabelle. Who she definitely was not. She was Mrs. Lépine, a matronly widow who could do as she pleased. Couldn't she? Just this once. Belle tried to steady her fluttering pulse. This was the tamest of adventures. She and Sir Renaissance Painting Come to Life were strangers who need never cross paths again.

What harm could come from enjoying a moment or two of his company?

# CHAPTER 2

Calvin McAlistair immediately regretted gesturing at the empty chair on the other side of his small dining table.

He'd chosen the smallest table in the farthest corner specifically to avoid being forced to speak to anyone. Managing awkward small talk was painful enough with acquaintances. With strangers, it was impossible. Already his body tensed and his mind emptied of anything clever to say.

But though he had the social abilities of a block of marble, inside he knew all too well what it was like to gaze about and realize one did not belong. That there was no place here for you, and never would be.

The young woman he'd gestured to, on the other hand, did not appear familiar with the sensation of not having a place at the table. Even before her eyes had widened and her pretty forehead lined with disbelief, then consternation, it had been obvious from the moment she'd swept into the posting house that she expected to be welcome anywhere.

Soft brown hair, swept high. Cheeks flushed with good health rather than chapped from the cold. Gorgeous carriage dress of olive bombazine, trimmed with golden Spanish puffs and a double row of intricate matching crepe. Sarcenet-lined fur wrapping-cloak, combined with an enormous matching pelerine to guard against the winter weather.

In other words, she was the sort of woman his mother might have worked for, not the sort of woman who took her meals with common folk like Calvin McAlistair.

Despite his attire, he was no gentleman.

But it was too late to take back his reckless act of kindness. The elegant young woman glided his way, a hesitant smile on her pretty lips.

Calvin was more than hesitant. He was a rash, regretful curmudgeon who enjoyed the anonymity of large crowds, but vastly preferred solitude. He should have taken his meal in his room. Then she could have the entire tiny table to herself, and he would not be forced to spend the next quarter hour in increasingly awkward levels of hell.

But no. He'd already ordered his food, and he'd extended the silent invitation to come and disturb him.

She was here.

"Thank you." Her voice was confident, cultured, as rich as honey. He could almost taste each syllable on his tongue. She paused next to the empty chair.

Calvin did not leap up to pull it back from the table for her. He did not want to feel the rich fabric of her skirt brush against his stiff body or catch a hint of some flowery perfume as she sank gracefully into her chair.

Making it through his meal would be challenge enough.

"Mmphh," he said gruffly. He could not quite bring himself to say *my pleasure*.

She floated down into her chair like a feather nestling in the crook of a tree.

Interactions such as these were torture, not out of fear of rejection, so much as the certainty of embarrassing himself. He did not know what to say to a refined lady in a posting house dining room, and preferred saying nothing at all rather than mortifying them both with inescapable awkwardness.

Now that she'd sat before him, they were both trapped. There would be no running away until the food was ordered and consumed. Even if he wolfed down his mutton pie in the space of a breath, politeness dictated he remain in his seat until she, too, had finished eating.

The hesitant smile was back on her lips. "I'm... Mrs. Lépine."

"McAlistair." The word came out easily.

In fact, his muscles had relaxed considerably and the hardness in his stomach had nearly vanished. *Mrs.* Lépine was the best possible name the beautiful stranger could have.

She was obviously respectable—one glance at her expensive carriage dress indicated that much

13

—and a respectable married lady would not be in the least concerned with what kind of impression Calvin happened to make.

"Are you here on holiday?" she asked politely, her cultured accent slightly jarring.

"No."

He was here on business. Mostly. Which was another reason why he should have taken his meal upstairs in his room. He would not come downstairs again until he was ready to leave. Calvin did not have time for distractions, even temporary ones that smelt of lavender.

Why *did* she smell like lavender? She had just arrived; he'd been watching. He watched everyone, took note of everything. The back of her traveling costume was wrinkled. She had a driver, a maid who'd fallen sick. She should smell of long carriage rides, not lavender.

Belatedly, he remembered it was his turn to ask a question. He went with the same one she had chosen.

"Are you here on holiday?"

"Yes." Her hazel eyes lit with warmth, elevating her features from beautiful to luminous. "We'll spend the Yuletide visiting friends and family."

He did not have to ask who "we" was. She was Mrs. Lépine. "We" meant she and her husband, the imprudently absent Mr. Lépine.

Calvin would never find himself in such a predicament, because Calvin did not intend to marry. A wife would get in his way, and he in hers. They would be forced to have awkward dining conversations like this three times a day. True, some married couples never saw each other save for the occasional nocturnal visit, but Calvin saw even less point in leg-shackling oneself to someone one had no wish to spend time with.

Oh, he understood why the aristocracy did so. Heirs and such, the passing down of titles and entailed estates, the strategic alliance to increase land or political connections. After the obligatory begetting of sons, each party was free to discreetly do as they pleased. Many lords kept the same mistresses they'd had since before the wedding.

Calvin did not need to bother with any of that. No title, no land, no estate, no link to politics. If he wanted a mistress, he could just get one, and skip the bit about lying to his wife about it. Being a common bachelor was simple and straightforward. Having no friends and family to visit, even better. No strings at all, just as he liked it.

"McAlistair," she said slowly, as if tasting his name the way he tasted all of her honey-rich words. "Are you Scottish?"

"No." Maybe. Probably. It was none of her business. He turned the tables back on her. "Are you?"

"Am I... Scottish?" She leaned back. "I'm Mrs. _Lépine_."

He shrugged. "You're not French."

Her face flushed crimson. "How... I... My husband..."

The serving girl appeared, rushed and out of breath. She looked at Mrs. Lépine. "Pie and ale?"

Mrs. Lépine darted a startled look at Calvin.

"I've already ordered," he told her. "Pie and ale."

"You, madam?" prompted the serving girl.

"Er," said Mrs. Lépine as if they were all speaking a different language. Perhaps she *was* French. "Is there a menu?"

"Yes," the serving girl replied impatiently. "Pie and ale if you're hungry, no pie if you're not."

"She'll have the pie and ale," Calvin murmured.

The serving girl bobbed her head and spun away without another word.

"Thank you," Mrs. Lépine said. "I thought... I don't know what I thought."

"You thought there would be choices," Calvin said dryly. "And usually you would be right. But when the dining room is this busy, the kitchen makes one meal in order to feed the guests with as much haste as possible."

It was the longest speech he could remember making to a stranger. Nor was the topic a particularly interesting one.

But Mrs. Lépine grinned at him as if they were old acquaintances sharing a private jest.

Calvin's heart beat uncomfortably fast.

"Have you stayed here long?" she asked.

"A few days."

Eight, to be exact. Tomorrow he would depart for a meeting that would change his life forever.

He hoped.

But before he met with the investor, he needed to finish the new prototype. That was why he had chosen this posting house. Close enough to be a convenient distance from his meeting. Far enough that he need not fear running into his business partner before the prototype was ready.

Far enough for *Calvin* to get ready. Days of haggling with his business partner over the best way to present their secret project awaited him, followed by the most awkward conversation ever, in which he and his partner attempted to convince a potential investor to part with his money in order to fund a speculative venture.

All of which meant he should not be sitting at a cozy table, making idle talk with a married lady. Perhaps it wasn't too late to have the serving girl send his pie and ale up to his room. Unconscionably rude perhaps, but it wasn't as though Mrs. Lépine longed for Calvin's company in particular. They were strangers and would remain so. Once he exited the dining room, he would never lay eyes on her again.

"Ale." The serving girl thunked two pints onto the table and disappeared.

Mrs. Lépine stared at her glass of frothing ale as though she had no idea what she was meant to do with it.

Calvin lifted his and held it up toward her. "May the pies arrive as fast as possible."

She burst out laughing and clanked her glass with his, her hazel eyes merry. "I'm being horribly awkward, aren't I? A thousand heartfelt apologies, Mr. McAlistair. I'd like to blame the long journey, but the truth is, I've never been in a situation such as this, and I find myself uncertain what to do or say. You are a perfect gentleman to let me stumble about so without a word of complaint."

He stared at her.

Mrs. Lépine thought *she* was being horribly awkward? And *Calvin* a perfect gentleman?

"*I've* never been in this situation either," he blurted out, exactly unlike how a perfect gentleman would do.

Mrs. Lépine all but melted in obvious relief. She brought her glass back to his with a conspiratorial grin. "To two hopelessly lost souls sharing a delightfully awkward supper together."

It had never occurred to Calvin that awkwardness could be delightful, but if ever it were to be true, it was at this moment, right here with her. He clinked her glass. "To pie and ale with a stranger."

But already the word no longer fit. The sharpest edges had worn away. He no longer felt prickly and uncomfortable. Or rather, he still did, but in a new way. The prickles fluttered in his stomach, rather than crawled upon his skin. His discomfort came not from the desire to flee, but the realization that he no longer wished to. He hoped the kitchen took twice as long with the pies.

"This is my first time in Houville," Mrs. Lépine confessed.

"Mine, as well." He hesitated, then added, "I cannot tell you much about it. I haven't left the posting house since I arrived."

"I shan't have an opportunity to go exploring, either. I didn't mean to stop here. As soon as my maid is well enough to travel, we'll be off."

Calvin did not ask to where. The Christmas village of Cressmouth was an obvious choice, but the Yuletide was still a fortnight away. Perhaps the reason she'd inquired about Scotland was because she was heading there. Or maybe she was en route to London. She looked the part.

"I wish your maid good health."

"As do I." Her tone was so fervent, one might be forgiven for thinking a family member had fallen ill, rather than a servant. She took a sip of ale and wrinkled her nose. "Is it meant to taste like this?"

The corners of his mouth twitched.

"The ale is actually nice," he admitted. "I suspect many of the dining guests are local residents who've come specifically because of the ale."

She took another sip, swished it in her mouth for a moment, then swallowed with a grimace. "Will it grow on me?"

"Do things tend to?"

She tilted her head to one side as if this were a fascinating question she had not previously considered.

"Some things," she said at last. "The best ones are like honeysuckle. By the time you notice, they've bloomed, and you're glad they've taken over your façade."

Calvin blinked at the image. He often thought in terms of façades and pretty armor. It was the reason he always dressed as though he was off to promenade with the *bon ton* in Hyde Park. At a young age, he had learnt that the easiest way to avoid unwanted questions was to appear highborn enough that it would be impertinent to ask.

Mrs. Lépine was likely being metaphorical.

"Have you honeysuckle growing on your house?" he asked.

She shook her head. "Red brick. It's... When I'm there, I'm usually somewhere else. At a window looking out, or carrying my favorite paint set off to—"

Her cheeks flushed, and she took a sip of ale rather than finish her sentence.

"Do you paint?"

She waved this off. "All ladies are forced to dabble in watercolor during their youth. What about you?"

"Do I watercolor?"

"I don't know your vice. That's why I'm asking."

He wasn't certain whether it was more intriguing that she'd grouped herself in with "all ladies" or that she considered watercolor a vice.

"I have no vices." None that he was willing to mention. "Except for opium-eating, pig wrestling, and the politesse not to mention a frothy mustache on a supper companion's top lip."

She let out a choked giggle. "Have I froth on my lip?"

"You make it fetching," he assured her. "If Ackermann were to walk by, he'd sketch you on the first page of the next repository."

"In that case..." She lifted her ale to her mouth and held it to her lip for a moment too long. When she returned her glass to the table, the hint of froth below her nose was now a lopsided swath of bubbles. "All better?"

"Your frothy whiskers are undetectable." He pretended to scrutinize her. "Unless I'm looking at you."

"Pie." The serving girl slid two steaming platters onto the table. "You've got froth on your face."

Calvin and Mrs. Lépine burst into laughter.

The serving girl had already moved to the next table.

"She doesn't understand high fashion," Mrs. Lépine whispered.

"No one ever does," he said sadly. "It's a curse."

"I hope this pie is the cure. It smells divine."

"They've excellent pies here," Calvin admitted. "My favorite is the minced meat. I shan't be at all offended if we're too busy shoveling food into our froth-adorned mouths to have time for conversation."

"I shan't be offended either..." A shy smile curled up one side of her lips. "But I would be disappointed. It turns out I'm glad there were no free tables in the dining room. I've been enjoying sharing this ale together."

"You hate the ale," he reminded her.

"True." She set down her glass. "Then it must be the fine company I like so much."

The back of Calvin's neck flamed with heat. Thank heavens for the pompously overblown neckcloth exploding from his throat. Mrs. Lépine would not see him blush like a schoolboy.

He wasn't certain precisely when it had happened, but he'd at some point forgot his awkwardness entirely. He hadn't realized that forgetting one's awkwardness was a phenomenon that could even occur.

"I suspect," he said gruffly, "I'm only fit company when with the right person."

"You charming flatterer." She blotted her lip with a serviette, eyes twinkling. "If we've determined anything, it is that I am the wrong person to take anywhere. If the pies hadn't arrived when they did, who knows what silly mischief we'd have got up to next."

That sounded... marvelous. *She* was marvelous.

No, no. This could not stand. He picked up his cutlery and fixed his gaze on his pie. He did not have time for a distraction, even one as fetching as Mrs. Lépine.

His future depended on it.

# CHAPTER 3

*B*y her final morsels of pie, Belle was not ready for the meal with Mr. McAlistair to end.

What was it about him? He was obscenely attractive, yes, but Belle was not new to attractive men with exquisite tailoring. London ballrooms were rife with dashing rakes with inflated opinions of their irresistible magnetism.

Mr. McAlistair did not appear to be attempting to charm her. If anything, lack of artifice was his most charming trait. He did not seem to be trying to convince her of anything. Not even to linger at the table a little while longer.

"Well," he said, when not a crumb remained. "I assume you are as busy as I am. Thank you for such charming company."

Belle was not as busy as he was, although she was now dreadfully curious to know just how he spent his time.

Her time was spent being a lady. Morning calls, a promenade in Hyde Park, then a supper party, followed by the opera or a ball... Perhaps she'd sneak away for a moment to paint. Or if her mother saw her, she was doomed to dedicate half an hour of the day's best light to studious embroidery in the front parlor, to increase their already inexhaustible supply of delicate whitework handkerchiefs.

It was busy, but it was not *busy*. It was fifteen hours of eating, drinking, and changing clothes, followed by a good night's sleep. It was neither meaningful nor particularly exhausting, and Belle would not have interrupted this easy meal with Mr. McAlistair to hurry back to any part of her very important normal life.

She tried not to let it sting that he did not feel the same. If he'd known she was Lady Isabelle... but of course she did not wish to trap him here with her title. She'd hoped he'd want to linger for *her*.

Foolishness. Every man who had ever sought her presence did so due to proximity to a title, a desire for her dowry, or because he was a paid servant obliged to dote on her every whim. She was Mrs. Lépine now. What had she expected?

"I understand," she said smoothly, rising to her feet before he had a chance to. "I am very busy as well. I must return to my routine."

The latter, at least, was true enough. Although she had the mantle of Independent Widow to hide behind, maintaining her respectability was paramount no matter what one's marital status. Pie and ale had been diverting, but it was time to quit

Mr. McAlistair's fine company and have a maid or a footman escort her to room number eighteen.

She glanced about for a maid or footman.

She found neither.

The dining room was not as crowded as before, although still only staffed by the same sole serving girl.

Belle cleared her throat the next time the girl dashed by.

The serving girl did not slow or in any way indicate she had discerned any special meaning from the loud sounds coming from Belle's throat.

Instead, she made six more trips between the bar, the kitchen, and the tables, delivering ten pies and twenty ales faster than Belle could produce a serviceable chain stitch with needle and cloth.

Food and drink delivered, the serving girl materialized before Belle without the need of a second discreet throat-clearing.

"Yes'm?" Her tone and restless gaze implied Belle had approximately ten seconds to make her requests known.

"Is there a maid?" she asked quickly. "Or a footman?"

The serving girl made a slow blink. "Oh, your trunks, of course. Yes, they're up in your guest chamber. The kitchen opens at half past six every morning. Anything else?"

"Is a maid or footman here now?" Belle tilted her head toward the exit. "To help me to my room?"

The serving girl darted a glance over her

shoulder at the window to the kitchen before answering. "What is the number of your chamber?"

Belle lowered her voice so no one else would overhear. "Eighteen."

"Ah, eighteen." The girl repeated the number without altering her volume. "Third floor, left-hand side, second-to-last door. Is that all?"

"Another ale," shouted a male voice.

"Make it a round for the table," called another.

"I just..." Belle plucked at her fingers. "When might someone be available to escort me?"

The serving girl stared at her as if she'd never before heard that series of words strung together like that.

"I'll do it," Mr. McAlistair assured the girl. "Go on. You're busy."

Belle pressed her lips together tight to keep from pointing out that the *reason* an unaccompanied woman required an escort to her rented chambers was so it did not look as though she were slinking off to spend a torrid evening with a man she'd met an hour earlier. Independent Widows had reputations to mind, too.

But there was no maid, no footman, and the serving girl was already off filling new jugs of ale. She was just as busy as Mr. McAlistair professed to be.

"Never mind me," she told him. "I can find room eighteen on my own."

"I've no doubt. But you might as well follow me." He held up a brass key. "I'm in nineteen."

Of course he was.

She did not take his elbow—not that he'd proffered it—and fell into step in as respectable a distance as possible, given two people climbing the same set of narrow stairs side by side. In other words, the twilled skirt of her silk traveling dress kept brushing against his muscled calves, while his light scent of bergamot and sandalwood seeped into her very bones, like a luxurious steamy bath in the springtime.

*That* was what she needed. A nice, long, solitary soak, to wash the day's highs and lows from her hair and remind herself just who and where she was.

When they reached the third-floor landing, she gave a crisp, "Good night, Mr. McAlistair," as if she had not spent the past ten minutes deeply inhaling his intoxicating scent, and set about opening her door.

His room was next door. The furthest guest chamber on their side of the corridor. He would be right on the other side of their shared wall.

She wished she did not know that.

"Good night, Mrs. Lépine," came his delicious, low, gravelly voice.

Belle flung herself into her room, shut the door, and collapsed against it until her pulse returned to a sedate pace.

She was being silly. Father would say of course she was being silly; all females were silly. Mother's eyes would go a little hard, and she would counter that their daughter was not silly, just... peculiar. Belle had been an odd fish since birth. They should know what one could expect of her by now.

None of which was helpful. Their lack of faith that she could be anything other than a pretty ornament only made her wish to prove them wrong all the more.

She straightened her spine. Although she would never confess that she'd spent a day or two disguised as a widow of means, Belle could take this opportunity to prove to herself that she could absolutely be capable and independent.

Mrs. Lépine could do anything.

Beginning with calling a bath.

Belle glanced about the chamber in dismay. Mrs. Price had not exaggerated when she'd warned the last room was the smallest one. It contained a narrow bed, a slender table just wide enough for a bowl and pitcher, one lackluster window...

And all four of Belle's traveling trunks.

"There's always room for a bath," she muttered to herself, and tugged the worn bell pull hanging between the cramped bed and the small table.

What there wasn't room for was Ursula. Belle hoped her maid was comfortable in the sickroom. Even if she gave Ursula the bed and Belle slept on the worn floor between the trunks, there was little she could offer Ursula in the way of comfort in this tiny room. At first light, Belle would visit the sickroom to check on Ursula and ensure she was fed properly and had books and magazines or anything else she desired.

In the meantime, Belle simply had to survive the night. Alone.

Whilst she awaited a servant to heed her call,

she set about pushing her heavy trunks against the walls to create more space. A *lady* would have waited for a footman to do such a task. Mrs. Lépine was not so helpless.

Trunks thus arranged, Belle pressed her ear to her door to listen for footsteps. How long had it been since she'd rung the bell pull? Ten minutes? Fifteen? This wasn't like at home, she reminded herself. Nor was it anything like Marlowe Castle, where most travelers to Cressmouth spent their holiday. Perhaps all the staff were busy assisting other guests. It was a full house, was it not? Mrs. Lépine would be patient.

And Belle would use the unexpected time to paint. She pulled her traveling easel from her trunk of art supplies and locked it in its upright position. Instead of canvases, she'd brought thick sheets of Arches gelatin-sealed paper—perfect for dashing off a quick watercolor of a lively outdoor scene.

She peeked through the curtains to see what delights awaited her artist's eye.

Bricks. Bricks awaited. Her window was six feet from the building next door. She could reach out and join hands with the neighbor opposite, if the windows had lined up. Instead, she had a view of absolutely nothing, blurred slightly by the falling snow, and the growing accumulation of frost creeping from the perimeter of the window.

She dropped the curtain and turned back to her easel. Just because she always painted outdoor scenes did not mean she literally had to be looking at one while she painted. She had an imagination, didn't she? Mrs. Lépine would not allow a lack of sweeping views to suppress her art.

Neither would Belle. She glanced about for a stool or chair before remembering there was none, then dragged her easel over to the bed and perched on the edge of the mattress.

It squeaked.

She froze. Had Mr. McAlistair heard the squeak of her mattress? Well, what if he did? These were bedchambers full of people sleeping in beds. Mr. McAlistair might be slipping into his just on the other side of the wall.

"Do not think about that," Belle told herself sternly. "It is of no interest to you what sort of nightclothes Mr. McAlistair might be donning at this very moment."

In fact, she would do well not to have any further contact with him. What would be the point? It could lead nowhere, and besides, he was a very busy man. She would put him right out of her mind for the rest of her short stay in Houville.

Footsteps sounded in the hallway, followed by a soft knock. Finally, she could order a hot bath! Belle hurried to the door and threw it open wide.

No one was there.

Had she imagined the footsteps? Frowning, she stepped into the corridor.

Mr. McAlistair stood two yards away, accepting a large parcel from a maid.

"I'm sorry, sir," the maid was saying. "This arrived hours ago, but it got set aside during the supper rush and I only just now remembered."

"Thank you." Mr. McAlistair dropped a coin

into the woman's hand. "I've only just arrived back to my chamber myself."

He glanced over the maid's shoulder and trapped Belle in his dark gaze.

Her cheeks flushed with heat.

"Er," she said. "I wasn't eavesdropping. Well, not on purpose. I had rung my bell pull some time ago, and..."

Her words trailed off. There was no chance of her mentioning taking a bath in Mr. McAlistair's hearing.

"How can I help you, ma'am?" asked the maid.

Now that she stepped closer, Belle could see the girl was much younger than she'd first seemed. Exhaustion lined her face and cast purple shadows beneath her eyes.

She waited until Mr. McAlistair carried his parcel into his chamber before responding to the maid's question.

"Can you please have someone bring up a hot bath?"

The maid squinted at her. "Tonight?"

Belle nodded. "I would have called for one sooner, but I was famished when I arrived, and I..."

The girl made a pained expression. "I'll tell the footmen at once, but we're down two maids and a hall boy, thanks to the influenza—"

"*Two* maids?" Belle repeated. "I thought it was only one, other than my own."

"It was one, until just past twilight, and we'll be lucky to survive the night without adding one more to the list. Your bath will be up as soon as possible, but you might have to wait a few hours."

A *lady* would demand a bath at the earliest convenience, and wait up all night for it if she had to —likely because she'd be up all night dancing.

Mrs. Lépine, however, would not seek to add to a problem.

"Do you know what?" Belle rooted in her reticule for a coin and pressed it into the maid's hand. "Forget about tonight. Can you please see that a hot bath is brought up in the morning? Anytime after eight will do."

The girl's eyes widened at the sight of the gold crown in her palm. "Yes, madam. I'll see to it myself, madam. Have a very good night indeed!"

Belle watched in pleased amusement as the maid dashed off down the corridor and clattered down the stairs as if afraid Belle might change her mind about the vail and switch the crown for a penny.

Only when the girl was out of sight did Belle realize there was no chance of undoing the rear closure of her expensive traveling dress without an extra pair of hands.

"Wait!" She sprinted toward the stairwell in panic, but it was too late.

The maid was gone.

Belle clenched the wooden banister until her knuckles paled white. There she went again, *thinking*. She'd thought to be considerate of the servants in general, and kind to this maid in specific, but she hadn't thought about the four layers of clothing she couldn't undo by herself.

Could she do anything by herself? It was so hard not to get discouraged. She'd been Mrs.

Lépine for all of two hours, without a maid for the first time in her life, and already she was blundering and helpless. Just when she'd promised herself she could prove how capable and independent she could be if given half a chance.

Throat pricking with frustration, she turned from the stairs—

To find Mr. McAlistair standing just outside his bedroom door.

The parcel was gone. He was still in his evening dress, looking every inch the perfectly groomed Town rake on the cusp of taking a ballroom by storm.

Belle, no doubt, looked like a ragged mop in a fancy gown.

"May I be of service, Mrs. Lépine?"

It was his kindness that made her throat swell and her eyes sting. She'd humiliated herself enough in the past few moments. She would not compound the mortification by admitting her failings to him.

"No, thank you," she said as pertly as she could, though she could not make herself look him in the eyes. "I'm exhausted, Mr. McAlistair. I'll bid you a good night."

She made her way as far as the threshold to her rented chamber before she heard his voice again.

"Would you like some help with those fastenings?"

"No!" She spun to face him in horror, her heart clanging in embarrassment. How had he known? "All is well, thank you. I'll deal with my fastenings myself."

"You'll deal with a thin row of buttons down your spine yourself," he said in the same disbelieving tone her father might have used for, *You think you can do sums in your head?*

Father was wrong. Belle could absolutely do sums in her head.

Mr. McAlistair was right. The only way out of this gown was with the help of a lady's maid or a pair of shears.

"I'm not inviting myself into your bedchamber," he said quickly.

The thought hadn't crossed Belle's mind, but now that he'd put it there, she was fairly certain the catching of her breath had less to do with alarm at the idea of him touching her and more with the wonder of what his hands might feel like, brushing against her skin.

"N-no," she croaked. Definitely not an avenue she wished to pursue.

"We could stand out here in the corridor," he offered. "I could loosen it enough for you to manage the rest yourself."

That would be infinitely helpful... and unforgivably embarrassing. Even under a pseudonym, there was no possibility of Belle allowing a man to partially undress her in public.

Or in private, she reminded herself hastily. Mr. McAlistair's strong hands weren't coming anywhere near the fastenings of her dress.

"I enjoy sleeping in my gown," she blurted out. "A maid will help me in the morning."

He lifted a handsome shoulder. "As you wish."

But as Belle laid stiffly atop her unfamiliar bed

with her stays' strips of whalebone digging into her flesh, what she wished for most was not her maid or a bath or even the feel of Mr. McAlistair's fingers grazing her spine.

She wished he could think of her as independent and capable.

# CHAPTER 4

*B*elle did not bounce out of bed in the morning. She couldn't bounce anywhere.

The whalebone stays dug into her skin and she'd been both too uncomfortable and too nervous to move, lest she ruin her gown. The traveling dress had been designed for a sedate carriage ride, not the nocturnal flailing of a restless sleeper. She could not risk rending the fabric. Possessing enough coin to commission a new wardrobe was no help when she couldn't even rid herself of the dress she had on.

Should she have accepted her handsome new acquaintance's offer of help? No, definitely not. She could manage on her own. Or rather, with the maid who had promised to send up a hot bath in the morning. Belle's muscles ached at the thought of a nice long soak.

"Soon," she mumbled to herself.

What time was it? She glanced about for a clock, but there was none. Blearily, she stumbled to her reticule and fished out her pocket watch. A quarter to seven. No wonder it was still dark. The sun would not fully rise for another hour.

She tugged the bellpull to alert the maid that she had awoken early and was ready for her bath, then pushed open the curtain covering her small window. Most of the glass was etched with frost, but enough light filtered through to recognize falling snow.

Perhaps children would be playing in the square. Did Houville have a square? Belle knew little to nothing about this small village. If Ursula was feeling better, perhaps they could have a stroll after breakfast before heading on to Cressmouth. She and Ursula both enjoyed exploring the parks and gardens of London. It would be heaven to stretch their legs before piling back into the carriage.

Oh, how Ursula would laugh when Belle told her of her troubles! Ursula would say, *Now you see how indispensable I am!* but of course Belle had always known. They had been inseparable since long before Belle's come-out. Not just with the arranging of hair and the constant changing of gowns. Ursula was her companion, her chaperone, her friend. Today was the first time Belle woke up all alone. At home, Ursula slept in the adjoining chamber, but here, the only person on the other side of the wall was...

Mr. McAlistair. Whom Belle definitely was not still thinking about.

"I'll prove it," she said to the empty room.

No—not to the empty room. She would proceed as if Ursula were here and could hear her, and perhaps then Belle wouldn't feel so alone and lonely.

"Whilst we await the bath, I'll paint you a picture."

She dragged the easel before the snow-fogged window. The building opposite was still just visible.

"We'll call it... 'Blank Brick Wall, Obscured by Frost.' Perhaps this is the watercolor that will make me famous."

She grinned to herself as she arranged her paper and paints. She hoped Ursula was feeling much better this morning, but if not, at least she would know she wasn't missing out on an incredible view from Belle's room.

Once they arrived in Cressmouth, she planned to paint hundreds of picturesque Yuletide scenes. Belle would be visiting her friend Angelica until her brother's Christmastide party began the following week, but she would still have plenty of free time. Angelica was a talented jeweler, and seasonal tourists composed the bulk of her business.

Belle was of no help in the workshop—Oh, how she longed to be useful!—and took herself off to the castle to paint and stay out of the way. Most of her paintings she donated to the castle, but her very favorites she tucked into the leather portfolio inside her art supplies trunk to carry back home. She had an entire wardrobe filled with scenes of happy moments Belle had glimpsed around her and captured with paint.

She swiped a wet brush across the page. This

study of red bricks blurred by falling snow would not win any awards, but at least it would give a chuckle to Ursula. She was the only person who ever saw Belle's art.

Well, the only person who knew it was Belle who had created it. A few years ago, Belle had worked up the courage to submit her work to several venues. She didn't seek a showing in the British Museum, but thought she might contribute to theatre advertisements or fashion periodicals or illustrating books for children.

Every one of the men she'd spoken to had laughed in her face without even opening her portfolio. That was, when Belle had procured an audience at all.

Did she fancy herself an artist? Tears of laughter glistened their eyes. She was no creative genius. She was Lady Isabelle, sister to the new Duke of Nottingvale. Of course, they'd find some scrap to print as a favor to His Grace if his ward insisted, but didn't the young lady have something else she could play at? Something that wouldn't waste everyone's time?

It was Ursula who had refused to allow Belle to give up hope. She'd pointed at the basket of dreaded embroidery and asked whether Belle intended to sew handkerchiefs for the rest of her life, or use the cursed things to wipe away her tears of hurt and rage and find some other way to succeed.

That was when they'd dreamt up the first pseudonym. "Lady Isabelle" would never be taken seriously, but "Mr. Brough" was a reasonably skilled recluse, whose housemaid handled his transactions for him. Belle insisted Ursula keep Mr. Brough's nominal earnings as compensation for her role in the ruse, though she wasn't certain Ursula had spent so much as a penny. Neither of them wanted for anything.

At least, not for coin. Belle had never managed to spend all of her monthly pin money when her father was alive, and when her brother inherited, his first act had been to double everyone's wages, including the pin money that Belle and her mother received. Without Father's gambling expenditures, the dukedom was flusher than ever. He could afford to spoil everyone rotten.

Mother was happy, the staff were happy, Belle was... restless. Painting hot air balloon bills for Vauxhall Gardens and advertisements for Astley's Circus helped to fill some of her time.

That was, when she wasn't attending endless Society events and minding her impeccable reputation. As much as Belle chafed at the constraints of the beau monde, it was the world she'd been born into. A flawless reputation was a young lady's greatest currency, and the one thing over which she had any control at all.

Whatever dubious value Belle ascribed to achieving other people's idea of "perfect," she would play the game to prove to herself that at least she was competent in that much. She couldn't lose her standing in the one place she actually belonged.

A knock sounded on the door. Belle nearly dropped her paintbrush in relief. She pushed the easel aside to make room for the bath and hurried to open the door.

It was not the maid from last night. It was a trio of footmen who looked barely old enough to shave. Though the lads' movements were in graceful synchronicity, they were clearly in a hurry to be on to the next task.

"Er..." She stepped back as they carried in the bath and filled it with steaming water. "Will the maid be here soon?"

One of the footmen jerked his head up. "What maid?"

"The one that helps with the bath?"

"We just helped," he pointed out. "Ring the bell when you're finished, and we'll retrieve it."

"But the maid from last night," she tried again. Oh, why hadn't she asked for the girl's name? "Is she still in attendance?"

"Sally?" He shook his head. "She's in the sickroom with the others. Dorothea seems to be improving, but the doctor says it could be days yet before any of the invalids rise from their beds."

"*Days?*" Belle repeated, aghast.

Poor Ursula. She would not have a stroll in the square this afternoon after all.

"Days," the lad repeated. "Not that they'd be going anywhere anyway, what with the snowstorm and all. Mrs. Price says we might not shovel ourselves out of here until the end of the week."

"Snowstorm?" she echoed faintly.

"Waist high by now, I reckon, with no sign of slowing. Not that there's a soul to spare for the shoveling. With so many maids ill with influenza, we're having to clean on top of our regular duties."

"Duties we ain't doing, George, with you standing about jawing," another lad pointed out dryly. "We got eight more baths to deliver, don't we? Come on, then."

"Anything else, madam?" asked the third, before all three lads disappeared into the corridor.

Belle's cheeks flamed, but she shook her head.

She could not possibly ask some strange footman to unbutton her blasted gown. A rumor like that would attract all the wrong attention. Nor had she any intention of sending away a fresh hot bath. She would find *some* way to get into it.

But how? She cast her gaze about the small chamber with increasing desperation. Three trunks overstuffed with her most fashionable gowns, none of which could be maneuvered without Ursula's aid, and one trunk of art supplies. Not a single thing that could help in these circumstances.

She leaned over the tub and let the steam caress her face. Was this it? Her secret daydream of one day becoming a wealthy independent spinster ruined forever because she couldn't even get out of her own dress to take a bath?

Her eyes flicked to the wall she shared with Mr. McAlistair.

*No.* She couldn't. Could she? Impossible. Scandalous. Even for a make-believe widow. Wasn't it?

She bit her lip. No one would know. Who would he tell? He didn't even know her real name.

Besides, he seemed... genuine. He might *look*

like a dashing, dissolute rake, but hadn't attempted to manhandle her last night when he'd first surmised her predicament. When she'd said no, he'd respected her decision, shrugged at her obvious folly, and disappeared back into his room.

He *must* be in his room, mustn't he? Or at least in the posting house. If the snow was too high for servants to leave, Mr. McAlistair wouldn't have been able to ride off to wherever he intended to go after this.

Whatever she was going to do, she had to do it soon. The bath was hot now, but it would not stay so forever.

It was just a row of buttons. She would survive this.

She sucked in a fortifying breath and marched next door to knock before she lost her nerve.

Gooseflesh crept up her clammy skin. This was a terrible idea. This was what happened when Belle thought she could think. Her pulse sped with mortification. What if he was downstairs in the dining room and the other guests peeked into the corridor and saw her like this, in yesterday's dress with her hair wild from the pillow?

She knocked before she lost her nerve.

His door swung open.

"Mrs. Lépine." The words were even and calm, as though half-hysterical women knocking on one's door at dawn was a perfectly normal occurrence.

Dear God, it was dawn.

"I'm sorry," she babbled. "I didn't mean to wake you."

43

"You didn't."

Of course she hadn't. Now that she looked at him properly, he was dressed and coiffed to perfection. If a Renaissance painting and a French fashion plate could bear offspring, it would look exactly like Mr. McAlistair. Nobody *woke up* this distractingly attractive.

All of which caused the words to tangle in her throat. She'd wanted him to be impressed by her, not to pity her, yet here she was, a wild-eyed wilder-haired dandelion puff, on the verge of shattering into a thousand fluffy clocks from the tiniest breath of air.

He crossed his well-tailored arms and leaned against the doorjamb. "May I help you?"

# CHAPTER 5

"*M*ay I help you?" Calvin arched his brows.

Perhaps Mrs. Lépine had nothing better to do this morning than stand in the corridor staring at him, but the scant time remaining before his presentation was becoming more precious by the hour.

He presumed Mrs. Lépine was at sixes and sevens because the silk-wrapped button closures down her spine could not unfasten themselves. But the same had been true last night, when she'd refused his help the first time.

They'd shared a lovely meal—the loveliest Calvin could recall having shared with anyone— and then suddenly Mrs. Lépine was no longer the friendly, open, teasing, happy woman she had been until the end of the pie. He could almost see her close up, her eyes looking away, her smile disappearing, her eagerness to be away from him, and her horror at discovering their guest rooms were on the same floor.

45

As someone who had been dreadful at social encounters for every one of his nine-and-twenty years, one might suppose Calvin had garnered some wisdom as to just what exactly had gone awry.

One would be wrong.

He had no data to parse because he had decided long ago that being a taciturn recluse was far better than continually risking rejection only to garner disappointment and embarrassment in return. He didn't need anyone else. He was perfectly fine just as he was.

And he did not have time for beautiful, hazel-eyed distractions.

"I know you don't want my help," he said with a sigh. "But it would be a shame to cause accidental damage to yourself or your dress trying to unbutton it on your own."

Not that she could. The olive bombazine had a capital silk warp with fine worsted weft, the craftsmanship exceptional. No one could remove it without help. Or without destroying the gown, which would be the greater tragedy. One rarely saw such artisanship in the flawless seams and exquisite detailing.

"Not in the hallway," Mrs. Lépine blurted out.

He stepped aside from his doorway.

She paled. "Not in *your* room."

He stepped forward.

"You can't come into my room," she stammered.

He stopped moving altogether. He did not know what she expected him to do, and was annoyed with himself for trying to fathom it out. She didn't want his company. She needed a favor. And she was making it bloody difficult to do that much.

In Mrs. Lépine's defense, she seemed just as flummoxed as he was.

"All right," she said at last. "I'll stand just inside my threshold, and you stand just outside. Then I won't be exposed to passers-by, and nor will I have invited a man into my room."

*Ah.* Of course. How had Calvin managed to forget *Mr.* Lépine?

Strangers enjoying a polite meal witnessed by three dozen chaperones was one thing. Allowing that stranger—rather than one's husband—to un-button one's gown in the corridor of a posting house... Poor Mrs. Lépine had every reason to be prickly.

"I understand," he said gruffly.

She flashed him a grateful smile and hastened to her chamber, positioning herself just inside the open doorway with her stiff shoulders facing Calvin.

He stepped up behind her, staying as far back as possible whilst still being able to reach the fastenings of her gown.

"There are eight buttons," he murmured.

She nodded. "Thank you."

He took a deep breath. Mrs. Lépine appeared to be holding hers. They could endure this. What were eight tiny buttons?

He brought his fingers to the first silk-wrapped pearl just beneath her nape and brushed a few stray mahogany tendrils to one side. She shivered.

As carefully as he could, Calvin released the first button. There. One unfastened. Only seven to go.

He lowered his fingers to the next button. "Will your husband be arriving soon?"

"What husband?"

"Mister... Lépine?"

"Oh." She let out a little self-conscious laugh. "He shall not. I am a widow."

Calvin's fingers froze at the second button.

A widow.

Not a married lady.

A widow clothed in bright olive, not the black of mourning or the gray of half-mourning. Mr. Lépine had been gone for well over a year, perhaps even many years.

Long enough for his widow to respond, *What husband?*

Calvin swallowed hard. He did not know what to do with this information.

Nothing. He would do nothing. He would un-button seven more silk buttons and walk away, just as he'd intended. Just because Mrs. Lépine had no Mr. Lépine did not mean Calvin did not have life-altering responsibilities to attend to, far away from his pretty neighbor.

Seven more buttons and he was gone.

"I'm sorry for your loss," he murmured, and unclasped the second button.

Did she just lean into his touch?

His fingers shook as he unfastened the third

button. More of her soft skin was now exposed. He tried not to notice.

When the fourth button unhooked, the ruffled tip of a chemise brushed against his fingers. Calvin's throat tightened. This felt less like a favor and more like a seduction with every newly exposed inch.

He was used to undressing people in his mind. It was a requirement of his profession. He needed to be able to see through their clothes, imagine them without, with something better.

But this wasn't his imagination. This was the curve of her spine, the texture of her skin, the flirty ruffle of a translucent chemise. He didn't have to imagine something better. He wasn't even certain he could.

"Next button," he rasped.

What number was this? Five. Don't look at her skin, look over her shoulder instead. No. Bad idea. Now he was looking at a bathtub, filled high with still-steaming water.

He was absolutely *not* to imagine a naked Mrs. Lépine reclining luxuriously in a pool of warm soapy water.

Five, six, seven, eight! Calvin's fingers flew down her spine, releasing each button as fast as his shaking fingers allowed. The sides of her gown flapped open, revealing delicate skin, more than he should ever see of her chemise, and the reinforced hem of the top of her whalebone stays.

"*There,*" he said, or maybe panted, or perhaps he just thought the word.

He leapt back and to one side, out of view of the waiting bath.

She turned to face him. "Thank you."

"It's always a pleasure," he croaked, and immediately regretted it.

Not *always*. Never. He was locking himself in his chamber and refusing to answer his door until he completed his project.

"When I'm finished with my..." Her cheeks flushed a becoming pink. She pressed a hand to her bodice to keep the unfettered neckline from falling open, and bit her lip. "When I'm dressed in a fresh gown, would you help me fasten it?"

No. He was very busy. She would just have to... sit right next door in a state of half-dress, while he attempted not to think about her.

"All right." What choice did he have? But he would not let her know how she affected him. "Knock hard. I don't hear distractions when I am working."

Was that too harsh? Was it not grumpy enough?

"I understand." She closed her door quickly, but not fast enough to obscure her whispered, *"Thank you."*

He marched directly to his room and locked the door.

Work. He was here to work. The knowledge that Mrs. Lépine was disrobing next door in order to slide into a warm, sudsy bath made absolutely no difference to him.

So what if there was no husband to consider?

*Calvin* was uninterested in the role. In any

role. He avoided other people whenever possible, and had no intention of changing. If he were to take a wife one day, it would be another solitudinarian like him. Someone with her own interests, who would not bother him, nor wish him to bother her. Save for shared nights in each other's arms, they would not be in each other's way at all.

If he ever found such a fellow hermit. Most women were social creatures who expected friends, family, parties and small talk with strangers. Calvin couldn't think of a worse hell. Why ruin both their lives? Such a woman would be disappointed to be his wife. Angry, resentful.

Calvin didn't want to have to upend his life to fit someone else's idea of the ideal husband. Such interactions gave him hives. He was happier on his own. He *liked* solitude. He wanted to keep it. He was never bored by himself. There was far too much work to do to have time for loneliness.

He would answer Mrs. Lépine's knock and button up her new dress, and that would be that. She could find someone else to play handmaid. Calvin had an empire to build.

He strode deeper into his suite, passing the closed door to his bedchamber and instead entering the small sitting room he had converted into his base of operations.

A single sofa lay against one wall. Calvin had dragged the two semi-matching wooden chairs to the opposite wall, where they were barely visible beneath piles of rich fabrics. Between the chairs was a small fireplace, before which he kept absolutely nothing. He could not risk a single spark marring any of his hard work.

Morning sun streamed through the large window on the final wall. Unlike the red bricks outside his bedroom window, this direction faced a sweeping panorama of snow-covered hills adorned with frost-tipped evergreens.

Calvin had only glanced through the pane once since his arrival. His interest did not lie in the out-of-doors, but rather the trunks of treasures he had arranged indoors. The best part about the window was not the view, but the influx of sunlight. He needed to take advantage of every hour of natural light possible.

He made his way to Duke, the tall, broad-shouldered wicker manikin modeling Calvin's latest prototype. He couldn't wait for Jonathan to see this one.

Jonathan MacLean was a clever business partner, a talented artist, and persuasive speaker. The gregarious Scot had not only convinced Calvin to agree to dedicating months of his life to this risky venture, but also captured the interest of a wealthy prospective sponsor, whose investment and influence would turn this project from a dream into reality.

Calvin grinned at Duke, and began adjusting the pins holding the lay figure's raffish evening wear in place.

Despite the elegant wickerwork figure's lordly title, the intended audience for Calvin's designs was not aristocrats, but ordinary men like him. Dukes and earls already had their preferred tailors, some of them famous like Schweitzer and Davidson, who outfitted dandies like Brummel.

Calvin's creations weren't bespoke designs customized to the individual client, but rather sophisticated but accessible styles meant to be produced on a grand scale and sold as-was in clothiers well off Bond Street. One could enter a millinery shop in Yorkshire or perhaps a draper in Cornwall and rent or purchase marvelous, already tailored, full evening dress for the monthly ball in one's local assembly rooms.

Or, if Jonathan were to be believed, he and Calvin would sell directly to customers all across the nation via seasonal catalogs, just as they now ordered books or seeds.

Men and women already thumbed through repositories such as Ackermann's and La Belle Assemblée to gawk hungrily at the magnificent styles they could never afford. Why not give them something they could?

Pins protruded from the corner of his mouth as he adjusted the fit of the manikin's waistcoat. Men were going to covet this style.

Calvin would create the designs and prototypes, Jonathan would sketch and color the advertisements. They'd employ local seamstresses and textile workers for the actual manufacturing, and the money would pour in like the tide. The "Fit for a Duke" line of men's apparel would be as popular as bread and butter by springtime. Aspirational fashion at affordable prices.

Although a fundamental tenet of their operation was *no custom orders*, for the discerning client all was not lost. The hems were sewn generously enough that each item could be taken out or in, as the wearer's body required. All material sumptuous, but sturdy.

If one did not have access to a tailor, perhaps one's wife or sister or the aspiring gentleman himself could arrange his own alterations. If it were not as neatly done as Schweitzer and Davidson did, who would know? The wearer would not be rubbing shoulders with actual viscounts and marquesses. He'd merely *look* like he could, in the eyes of his compatriots.

It would be enough.

The appearance of wealth held almost as much power.

Calvin knew this magic firsthand. His impeccable attire was the armor that protected him since he was a child. The thought that others might need it too had been the spark behind this project. For years, it had remained a favorite dream, until he'd confessed the idea to Jonathan.

Jonathan had not only seen the potential at once, he'd also outlined a dozen ways to make it even better. Calvin wanted to create affordable, aspirational fashion? Let's call the company *Fit for a Duke*, and present each offering as though it were a fashion plate. Calvin wanted to stay behind the curtain, perfecting the product but never speaking to prospective clients? Perfect! Jonathan *loved* meeting new people, and could sell hair combs to a bald man. They'd be off and running in no time at all.

Success was so close Calvin could smell it. His

longest, dearest dream, mere weeks from coming true. All he had to do was survive a painfully awkward in-person meeting with a wealthy investor, whose contribution—if Calvin's prototypes and Jonathan's sample advertisements were compelling enough—would determine whether *Fit for a Duke* launched to the stars, or sputtered out like the last gasp of a candle.

It *would* be good enough, damn it all. Calvin was unwilling to accept otherwise. The talent was there. The costumes were gorgeous.

He set his shears atop a tall stack of Jonathan's sketches. When they met in a couple of days to go over the latest prototypes, they'd choose the best sketches together. Jonathan would color each illustration to Calvin's specifications and arrange them like a fashion repository, presenting it to the investor as their inaugural catalog. Every household in England would recognize their names and the distinctive lettering of *Fit for a Duke*.

All Calvin had to do was create a few more immaculate designs, get to the meeting on time, and not say or do anything awkward to cock up the investment opportunity. His future and Jonathan's depended on everything going perfectly.

There was no room for even the tiniest mistake.

# CHAPTER 6

*B*elle never imagined that *looking presentable* would one day be a daunting challenge.

The first steps were deceivingly easy. Bathing herself was nothing new, nor was sliding on a linen shift. But that was as far as she could go.

Once Mr. McAlistair had unfastened her buttons, she'd managed to step out of her dress and slowly, painstakingly, loosened her stays, with a lot of wiggling and her arms twisted uncomfortably behind her to tug at the lacing.

Putting it back *on* by herself? Impossible. She did possess short demi-stays that laced in the front, but those were only used at home in the hottest days of summer, so of course she had not packed them for a winter holiday in the northernmost corner of England.

Asking handsome Mr. McAlistair to kindly fasten a few buttons was scandalous enough. She could not possibly stroll into a corridor with an expensive gown draped over one arm to request that the guest in the chamber next door first lace up her stays.

But if she went *without*... Belle gazed dubiously at her mint-striped sarcenet with its French ruff. Women *needed* their stays if there was to be any hope of the right silhouette. The boning didn't nip in one's midsection, but the ivory busk running down one's torso ensured proper posture and separated one's breasts, which were held improbably high by stiff, gravity-defying cotton half-cups. Without the stays to keep one's bosom in place, the carefully tailored bodice would be a disorderly, bouncing mess.

"Then mess it is," she muttered, as she slipped her day dress directly over her shift.

Without stays, her fashionable gown would look ill-tailored and unflattering. But she was Mrs. Lépine, not Lady Isabelle. Ill-tailored and unflattering was only a crime when one was the disappointing daughter of the Duchess of Nottingvale. An independent widow like Mrs. Lépine would not be bothered by something so trifling as a droopy bosom.

Besides, it wouldn't be for long. Even before morning tea or breaking her fast, Belle planned to go straight to Ursula to see how she was feeling. With luck, Ursula was much improved, and life could return to normal. All the same, Belle would take the watercolor she'd painted for Ursula in the hope of bringing a bit of cheer.

Heaven knew, Belle needed something to lift her spirits. Now that she was semi-clothed in a shift with no stays and an unbuttoned morning gown gaping open at the shoulder blades, the next question was what to do with her hair.

Ursula had always been the one to tame it and arrange it. Belle gazed hopelessly at her hand mirror. She'd dried her hair with the towel as best she could, but her tiny chamber did not contain a fireplace to sit beside. She dragged a comb through her long locks, so at least they weren't tangled, and then opened Ursula's traveling case of coiffure accoutrements.

Hair combs, diadems, and tiaras floated in a sea of hairpins.

What the dickens was Belle meant to do with all of that? The posting house wasn't a diadem or tiara sort of establishment. The diamond and pearl hair combs seemed equally out of place. The pins could secure any number of complicated interlocking braids or intricate twisting coiffures—*if* one had any notion how to do so.

Belle... did not.

With a sigh of frustration, she gathered all her hair in one big hunk, twisted it until it formed a knot, and then jabbed in pin after pin until the bun mostly stayed in place. It immediately listed to one side.

So much for her daydream of becoming a fashionable independent spinster. She'd been Mrs. Lépine for less than one day and was already a disaster. Her shoulders tightened. She closed the box of pins and strode to her door, then paused before her fingers touched the handle.

The only thing Belle hated more than feeling useless was for other people to think it about her, too. Yet the only way she could go downstairs to see Ursula was if she first ventured next door to beg Mr. McAlistair to button her dress.

She lifted her head high. A half dozen pins showered about her shoulders. Ignoring her increasingly lopsided hair, she pressed her lips together and marched out into the corridor to knock on Mr. McAlistair's door.

It took him longer than expected to answer. When the door swung open, he stared at her without comprehension for a moment, as if he'd forgot who she was and what she needed him to do.

Or as if he were a busy man with important things to do that Belle had just interrupted.

"This is the last time," she said in a rush. "I'm on my way downstairs to resolve this matter posthaste. If my lady's maid is still unwell, I shall employ another at once."

His brown eyes sharpened their focus. He took in her sagging hair, her sagging bosom, her sagging dress, and grimaced as if her crimes against fashion physically wounded him.

Her cheeks flamed with heat, but she held her ground.

"Turn around," he said gruffly.

She turned around, her heart pounding. Although he was to button her up, rather than unlace her, the brush of his fingers against her spine felt even more decadent and sensual than before.

It wasn't because she was attracted to Mr. McAlistair, she assured herself. This strange sensation was because she was missing a layer of protection. The thick cotton stays kept her torso immobile and her breasts molded in place.

It was the chill winter air in the drafty corridor that made her nipples pucker against the thin linen of her shift. It had nothing at all to do with the heat of Mr. McAlistair's body or the brush of his calloused fingertips against the gooseflesh of her bare skin.

"Six buttons," he said hoarsely. "This will go faster than last time."

Yes. Belle had removed all two dozen gowns from their traveling trunks in order to select today's dress based on the least number of buttons. It was an act of self-preservation. He hadn't even started yet and her flesh shivered in anticipation.

He gathered the loose flaps of her gown to the nape of her neck. "Hold this."

She reached up behind her neck to grab the twilled silk as requested, and instead accidentally caressed Mr. McAlistair's fingers.

He froze.

She froze.

Now they were holding hands in the most awkward way possible, with one of her elbows jutting high in the air.

"I'm so sorry." She let go at once and tried not to melt into a puddle of mortification.

"No, it's..." His free hand closed about her trembling one and guided her fingers back to the finely ribbed sarcenet. "Right there. I'll start at the bottom and be through in a trice."

She nodded, not trusting her ability to be coherent.

As before, Mr. McAlistair comported himself with the cool detachment of a total gentleman.

But he was not a gentleman. Despite his handsome face and impeccable attire, he had never been anywhere near Belle's social circles, or she would have heard his name before now. Clothes could lie. Look at her—she doubted her current state gave anyone the impression of a woman who was secretly a duke's daughter.

She didn't even seem like a marginally independent widow.

His hand covered hers lightly. "You can let go now."

She dropped her arm to her side. Probably her forearm should ache from having twisted at such an odd angle for so long, but all Belle could feel was the phantom sensation of Mr. McAlistair's warm hand gliding over hers.

"There." His soft breath tickled a stray hair at her nape. "All buttoned."

"Thank you," she said without turning around, and ran down the corridor to the stairs in the most embarrassingly unladylike manner possible.

Naturally, once she'd reached the second floor, she remembered she'd forgot the painting for Ursula, which meant Belle was forced to creep back up the stairs to her guest chamber and pray Mr. McAlistair was no longer in the corridor to witness her folly.

He was not. He was *busy*. He had more important things to do than stand about thinking about a disheveled widow with drooping everything.

Painting in hand, she made her way back down

the stairs toward the bar where she'd last seen the proprietress. Mrs. Price was not present, but due to the early hour, few guests were in the dining room, and the serving girl from the night before was able to greet Belle in short order.

"Sit at any empty table."

"I don't want breakfast." A loud rumble from Belle's stomach gave lie to her words. The kitchen's intoxicating scents nearly made her dizzy. "I'd like to see Ursula. Can you show me to the sickroom?"

"Absolutely not." The serving girl turned away.

Belle's mouth fell open. Had she just been dismissed? By a *servant*?

"You're Mrs. Lépine," she muttered to herself. "Mrs. Lépine enjoys being cut by serving maids. It's a hobby."

The girl glanced over her shoulder. "Did you say something?"

"Yes." Belle folded her hands. "Can you please tell me how Ursula is coming along and when I might see her?"

The girl's gaze softened with empathy. "She's over the worst of the symptoms. Because so many maids have fallen ill, Mrs. Price has forbidden all visits to the sickroom. That includes you, madam. There's no sense you taking ill, too. The influenza will pass in a few days."

"A few *days*?" Her stomach bottomed.

The serving girl laughed lightly. "Oh, it's not so bad. With the weather we've got, no one's going anywhere for at least that long, anyway."

"Is there..." Her pulse fluttered in panic. "Is

there someone I might employ temporarily in the meantime?"

The girl's eyebrows shot up with wry amusement. "If there was, Mrs. Price would have already employed her. Half of our maids are in the sickroom. You'd best take your meals down here, because there won't be anyone to carry trays up and down the stairs."

Belle sat down hard in the closest chair. No Ursula. No maid. No friend.

She was on her own.

"Tea or coffee?" the serving girl asked.

Neither.

"Do you have chocolate?" Belle asked hopefully.

The serving girl stared back at her flatly.

"Coffee," Belle said in defeat. "With milk and—"

"I'll bring you a plate."

Belle rubbed her temples. This was nothing like home. Lack of her ritual morning chocolate was the least of her concerns.

She'd never been alone before. Not properly. Ursula was always there at home, as well as dozens of other servants Belle had known since she was a child. Sometimes she took her easel outside to paint, but even that was done in busy places, surrounded by a crowd.

Most often, she went wherever her mother insisted. Teas, balls, gardens, theatre. Almack's on Wednesdays, Gunter's on Saturdays. It was the opposite of being alone. It was suffocating.

That was why Belle had so looked forward to spending a relaxing week with her friend Angelica prior to the start of her brother's Yuletide party. Angelica had loads of friends and family, but Belle wasn't required to put in an appearance at any given activity.

She could paint while Angelica worked in her jewelry shop, and then they could enjoy one of Cressmouth's many Christmas festivities or spend a lazy evening in Angelica's parlor, reading novels and drinking wine before the fire. She had *counted* on that week to restore her equilibrium before the obligatory whirl of Vale's party.

How Belle missed Ursula! Being snowbound in a posting house wouldn't be half so bad with a friend to talk to.

Belle's dream of independence was rapidly revealing itself to be a nightmare.

"Coffee." A tin pot and chipped cup appeared in front of Belle, along with a dram of milk and a plate of fruit, cheese, and toasted bread. "Your breakfast."

"*Wait.*" Before the serving girl could turn to go, Belle handed her the watercolor she'd painted. "Could you please see this is given to Ursula?"

The girl's eyes widened when she saw the paper contained nothing but a brick wall.

Belle's cheeks heated. "It's—"

"The third floor. The bit between rooms eighteen and nineteen." Impressed, the serving girl looked Belle over with renewed interest. She jabbed a finger at the paper. "I'm the reason those bricks chipped like that. Back then, me and Esther cleaned the guest rooms. One morning I leaned out of the window to—"

"Mildred!" called a male voice from the kitchen. "Does tea deliver itself now?"

"Hold your wool, Ezekiel," Mildred called back. "Wait 'til you see this!"

Mildred ran toward the kitchen, Belle's water-color in her hand.

She added milk to her coffee. It was difficult not to find it bittersweet that the first stranger to react positively to Belle's art was a serving maid reminiscing over a brick wall.

Belle's other dream, the one even closer to her heart than being an independent spinster—and just as unlikely an outcome—was to gather her favorite paintings together in a book. She'd been working on it for ages. It had gone through so many drafts that she would have more than enough content for an entire series of picture books: *Cressmouth at Christmas, Bath in springtime, High Season in London.*

The possibilities were endless.

The cost of publication was no object. She could publish a new collection every month if she pleased. The problem was... would it please anyone else?

Her work had already been rejected by every fashion repository or playbill designer in England. That was what had given birth to "Mr. Brough." If no one took Lady Isabelle seriously enough to let her paint an advert for a juggling clown, who on earth would wish to spend money purchasing an entire book of her paintings?

"Mr. Brough" could do it, of course. No one would blink an eye.

They also wouldn't know they were turning the pages of Belle's baby. She'd been painting her whole life, and yearning for recognition for just as long. But she couldn't bear being recognized as a national embarrassment.

Lady Isabelle, the coddled fool who thought she could paint.

Ursula had accused her of rarely allowing people close. Of Belle always keeping an easel or a pseudonym between herself and anyone who could hurt her.

Ursula wasn't wrong. It was easier that way. Safer. Infamy wasn't something Belle could ignore if she didn't like it. No matter how much money rattled in her purse.

She had to mind her reputation at all costs.

It wasn't just a matter of *looking* a certain way. Belle had to *be* a certain way.

Being the sort of lady a lord married was a currency far greater than gold. Society had certain expectations. Mother had even higher expectations. The longer Belle took to marry well, the more unsuccessful she looked in the eyes of her peers, and the more scathing her mother's lectures became.

How was Belle not a countess already? A duchess in her own right? A princess? She'd been bred for this like a blood-lined horse, for God's sake. If a common filly could do as it was trained, why couldn't Belle? From the moment she'd failed to be born a male, marrying well had been her *raison d'être*. When would she cease being a disappointment to her poor mother?

Belle shoved her empty breakfast plate away. Mother wasn't even here to scold her, and Belle could still hear every word.

She pushed to her feet. Mother needn't worry. Belle was slow, but she was dutiful. She would follow the path she'd been given and make her family proud.

It was why she was attending Vale's Yuletide party, rather than simply visiting Angelica. Her brother wouldn't be the only unwed lord in attendance. Perhaps in a less populated, relaxed, and friendly atmosphere like Cressmouth, Belle and some charming earl-marquess-prince would fall in love at first sight.

No, there she went again, being fanciful. *Thinking*, when she should not. How many times had Mother told her "love" was the chain binding the lower classes?

Duchesses didn't need *love*.

Countesses didn't need *love*.

Marchionesses didn't need *love*.

They needed a powerful husband with deep coffers. They needed an army of servants and countless acres of land and so many residences it was impossible to visit them all in a year. They needed to glare down their noses at Society with their heads held high because they were better than everyone else, and everyone knew it.

If Belle wanted to make her mother proud, she needed to stalk the Marriage Mart like a hunter. One didn't leave beauty *be*. One mounted its head on the wall in order to brag to all one's friends.

But first, Belle needed to survive the next few

days at the Hoot & Holly inn. Ursula was in the sickroom, along with half the other maids. The other staff did not have a moment to spare to deal with the sartorial whims of the widow Lépine. But Belle would still need to get in and out of her clothing.

Which left Mr. McAlistair.

He did not want to help her. He did not have time to help her. But he was all she had, and she was willing to pay handsomely for the favor.

He wasn't anyone of high social consequence, or she would already know his name. He dressed well, but so did Beau Brummell, and which dandy spent the mornings in a dressing room with Prinny, despite bearing no title?

Just as tellingly, Mr. McAlistair had chosen to take his holiday *here*, in the Hoot & Holly posting house, rather than continuing on to the next town, where guests enjoyed the sumptuous luxury of Marlowe Castle.

If she *paid* him for his time, she would be performing a favor in return.

She would simply have to otherwise keep her distance. No matter how solitary it felt all alone in an empty room. No matter how warm Mr. McAlistair's hands, or how sensuous his lips, or how broad and fit his shoulders were. Their dealings would be purely transactions. A few buttons for her, a few coins for him, then good-bye, *au revoir*, no further contact until the morrow.

It should be easy.

Even someone like Belle could manage that much.

She climbed the stairs to the third floor and bypassed her door to knock on his.

He answered the door with a shimmering hunk of golden cashmere over one shoulder and a sewing needle between his teeth.

Her eyes widened. She would get to the button agreement in a moment. First, she had to get to the bottom of... *this*.

"What are you doing?"

"Sewing."

Obviously. Perhaps this was the best of all possible scenarios.

"I can sew," she said quickly. "I can help you."

His expression was flat. "No, you can't."

It should not have hurt, but it did. He hadn't even seen the terrible destruction her embroidery had wrought upon innocent handkerchiefs, yet he could discern her ineptness just by looking at her.

"I can darn stockings," she informed him hotly. "And attach buttons."

He lifted a corner of the cashmere. "This isn't a stocking."

"What is it?"

The soft, rippling gold unfolded into a stunning waistcoat so beautiful it nearly hurt her eyes.

She gasped despite herself. "It's exquisite."

"I know." He tossed it back over his shoulder without changing expression.

He was right, damn him. If Belle even touched that fabric, it would fall apart in her hands. The best thing she could do for that waistcoat was keep her clumsy fingers away from it.

"Where did you find the pattern?"

"Pattern?" He repeated the word as though he'd never heard of the concept.

She gestured at the delicate cashmere. "For the waistcoat."

"Do you really want to know?"

No. She should not have asked. She should explain the button arrangement and then walk away. Flee, even. Secure her door with a key to keep her locked safely away from her impossibly handsome neighbor, with whom she would not spend a single second more time than absolutely necessary.

"Yes," blurted her traitorous mouth. "I want to know."

He gave a deep sigh as if he had feared that answer, then gallantly stepped aside. "Do come in."

# CHAPTER 7

*C*alvin cursed himself. Inviting Mrs. Lépine into his rented rooms was the opposite of avoiding distractions. It was inviting trouble.

And yet, from the moment she'd appeared at his door, inevitable.

He ushered her past his bedchamber and toward the small parlor he'd converted into a temporary workshop.

As soon as she stepped into the parlor, she shrieked and stumbled backward, straight into Calvin's chest.

He caught her, his arms sheltering her instinctively. Her hair was still damp from her bath and smelt of orange and nutmeg. He tried not to notice how well she fit against his body.

"What is it?" His cheek nestled against her head. "What has happened?"

The parlor looked as it always did. A bit messy, perhaps, with folded piles of fashionable prototypes and samples of expensive fabric laying on every surface, but he hadn't expected it to cause *terror*.

Mrs. Lépine let out a short, embarrassed laugh. "That man... I thought... When I glimpsed him from the corner of my eye..."

It was Calvin's turn to chuckle in embarrassment. "A thousand apologies for not explaining sooner. That's Duke, my manikin. He's a lay figure made of wickerwork, and the most patient model a tailor could have. He doesn't even mind when I poke him with a needle."

"*Are* you a tailor?"

It wasn't until she slid around to face him that Calvin realized Mrs. Lépine was still wrapped in his arms. He should let her go. He *would* have let go, if she had pushed away from him instead of turning toward him. His hands now rested at the small of her back. Her face was a mere hand's width from his.

"What was the question?" he rasped.

Her chin tilted up, bringing her lips even closer to his. All he would have to do was drop his head a few inches and his mouth could claim hers.

"You're a tailor? Out here? Who are your clients?"

"No clients," he managed. "The designs I'm creating are... a speculative experiment."

Her eyes were too close to his. He couldn't stop looking at them, drowning in them.

"You're very talented."

All she had seen was a waistcoat and a wicker manikin. She had no idea if Calvin was a talented clothier. Unless she wasn't talking about his designs. Then what would she mean he was talented at? Holding her close? Unbuttoning her gown?

He released her at once and turned to fiddle with the fireplace so she would not sense his consternation. "Would you like tea?"

"Tea?" she echoed blankly, as though she forgot the meaning of the word.

"I'll put the kettle on."

There. That was a calm, platonic, definitely-not-kissing-the-beguiling-widow action to take. Calvin had come to Houville to prepare for his presentation without disruption. He would serve his beautiful distraction a quick cup of tea, and send her on her way.

"You keep tea in your room?"

He glanced over his shoulder in surprise. "Don't you?"

She bit her lip. "My room hasn't even a fireplace."

He suspected that was not the full story, and cursed himself for wanting to know what the full story really was.

"I travel with everything," he said, rather than press for information. "When I'm working on a project, sometimes I don't leave the workroom for days on end. I've fallen asleep on that sofa as many times as the bed."

She glanced at the sofa with interest.

He deeply regretted mentioning beds at all.

"You mentioned you don't have clients," she said, and then paused as if Calvin would know what to say next.

He did not. The shrilling of the kettle saved

him from having to pretend to. He removed it from the heat, only to remember he had a month's supply of tea but only one cup and saucer. When he'd packed for "everything," he had not anticipated entertaining a pretty woman who could not remove her clothes without Calvin's help.

"I don't want tea," he announced, and shoved the saucer her way. The sooner she drank it and left, the sooner he could return to his work and life as usual.

She frowned. "Surely you—"

"I have only the one cup."

"Of course you do," she murmured, which made no sense at all. How many people did she know with only one teacup?

"Mrs. Lépine," he began.

"I'll pay you," she blurted out.

He blinked. "You'll what?"

"Just until Ursula recovers, or the snow melts, whichever comes first," she explained, as though that explained anything. She didn't touch her tea. She plucked at her fingers as if removing an invisible set of gloves. "You have no clients and I have no lady's maid. It's perhaps not perfect, but... I'll give you four guineas a day to continue buttoning me every morning and unbuttoning me at night."

Four guineas was more than the average maid or footman earned in an entire month.

Calvin would have unbuttoned her for free.

"Five guineas," said Mrs. Lépine, as though he had argued. "You are not a lady's maid, and I respect that. I shall also expect you to adhere to absolute discretion."

"Shall you?" he said, his voice dangerous.

"If it's not enough, just tell me your price," she said, as though he had answered an employment advert and was now being unreasonable. "Six guineas? Seven?"

Despite his fancy clothes, she saw him as someone to be purchased like a servant. Not a man who could give his word as a gentleman. Calvin's word carried no weight because he was no gentleman. He was a stranger to be pitied, or to be bought.

"The terms are," she continued as though he had dared to negotiate, "when we leave here, we do so as strangers. Not only won't anyone know you assisted in Ursula's place, you'll deny ever having met me at all."

"Will I?" Each word was cold and flinty. "Ten pounds a day, with a fifty quid minimum, paid up front."

There. Now she would know how it felt not to be trusted to keep one's word. Besides, fifty pounds was a ridiculous sum. The annual wage of a butler. Enough to commission two dozen serviceable day dresses with nary a button.

Not the sort of coin one offered a posting house guest so that one could pretend one had never met him without fear of the dirty secret being found out.

"Very well." She opened her reticule.

Who the devil gadded about with fifty quid in their reticule?

Someone who thought ordinary men like him

could be purchased and discarded, like a day-old newspaper.

"Why don't we sign a contract?" he asked with exaggerated solicitousness. "Will that set your mind at ease?"

Without waiting for a response, he set his writing slant atop one of his traveling trunks and put pen to paper.

"Ten per day... Fifty on signing... Buttons... Absolute discretion... Proceedings limited to Mrs. Lépine presenting herself at Mr. McAlistair's door... We the undersigned solemnly swear to never again acknowledge the other's existence once the roads clear or the maid resumes service, whichever comes first." He signed his name with a flourish and held out the plume. "Madame?"

"Thank you," she said without irony, and signed her name. "Now it is binding."

She placed five ten-pound notes onto his slant and picked up the "contract" by a corner, lest the ink smear.

Calvin didn't know whether it was better or worse that she didn't seem to realize how offensive it was to try and purchase a fellow guest like a servant.

No, not to *try*. She'd achieved it. The contract was in her hand.

Well, what did he care? He was fifty pounds richer. He hadn't been planning to *start* an acquaintance with Mrs. Lépine, much less continue on once they departed the Hoot & Holly. Which, hopefully, would be soon. The days before the meeting with the investor were dwindling, and he and Jonathan still needed to prepare the materials for their presentation.

Mrs. Lépine had granted Calvin a favor by limiting the scope of her distraction. They were to be neither friends nor lovers, but two temporary neighbors who briefly came together twice a day.

He should be thrilled at this turn of events. He fancied himself a misanthrope, did he not? A recluse, alone by design. Mrs. Lépine was just... Wasn't "lépine" French for "thorn?" A proper English rose; pretty to look at, painful to touch. He would stay on his path and leave her to hers. It was better for both of them.

She picked up her tea, realized it had gone cold, and set it back down in the saucer unsampled. "Will you show me more of your work?"

He stared at her. Would he *what?* She'd just paid a proper ransom to keep him in his place, and now she wanted a tour of his haberdashery? And Calvin thought *he* didn't know how to avoid awkwardness with other people.

Maybe... maybe Mrs. Lépine didn't know either. Maybe she was *worse.* Maybe what she needed most wasn't help with buttons, but kindness.

"It must be brief," he reminded her. "I'm very busy."

She nodded eagerly and set the contract on the sofa cushion next to her reticule.

How much blunt was left inside? A fistful of hundred-pound notes? Did she even realize he could not exchange her ten-pound notes for ready cash unless he visited the Bank of England in London?

Perhaps that explained Mrs. Lépine. She was from London. Her clothes indicated wealth, although Calvin of all people knew how little stock to put into a fine costume.

Her refined accent had been a better clue. Money wasn't something new she had married into, but rather something she had been born with.

Perhaps this was her first trip outside London. How *would* she know how everyone else lived? Her husband would have handled all financial matters. Or a man of business would have, Calvin supposed. Perhaps Mr. and Mrs. Lépine had been creatures of leisure.

Perhaps she had asked about Calvin's work not because she was interested in him or his art, but because she was bored, and he was the caged tiger in the menagerie.

"In short," he said as if concluding a long lecture, even though he had just begun. "This—" He pointed at his manikin. "—is the sort of evening dress one might wear for dancing at the local assembly. These—" He held up a few pieces that had been lying folded on one of the chairs. "—are different waistcoat fabrics and cuts, depending on the preference and body shape of the wearer. Those—" He gestured vaguely toward the other chair. "—are trousers with varying styles of straps, depending on the dimensions of the wearer's foot and the fit of his boot."

"These are beautiful." She gazed at the waistcoats in his hand with reverence, reaching out to touch one and then dropping her hand to her side just before her fingers could graze the fine material.

His chest swelled with warmth.

"But..." Her brow furrowed. "Wouldn't you know your customer's preferences and dimensions?"

"Not if all goes well," he said cryptically, then took pity on her confusion.

Telling her would change nothing. She would not start her own catalogue to compete with his, and even if she attempted to, the gambit would not work. Calvin might be ill at ease in social situations, but he was a skilled designer, and he knew it. Jonathan was his perfect complement; unable to sew a straight seam, but friendly, persuasive, with an eye for opportunities others would miss. Fit for a Duke would be the toast of England— provided the snow melted in time to make his meeting, and that the investor saw the true potential.

"It's pre-made apparel," Calvin explained. "One can have it tailored separately or wear each item just as it comes. The idea is to look like one is wearing expensive clothing without the money and time investment of a good tailor. Our ideal client won't even know what fashion to ask for. He just wants to be handsome."

"'Our?'"

"My business partner and me. This will be much too large an operation to run on one's own."

He hoped.

Mrs. Lépine was still frowning. "You don't want wealthy, fashionable patrons?"

"No," he said flatly. "I've no use for them, nor they for me. They have their own needs and resources. My designs are for the people who do not. I want to give people of middling incomes and nonexistent connections an opportunity they would not otherwise have."

She tilted her head. "Your aim is that, at any given country assembly, the local dairy farmer should be indistinguishable from the lord of the manor?"

"Exactly," he agreed without hesitation. "That's precisely it. Obviously, someone familiar with fashion can tell the difference, but such individuals are of no interest to me *or* to my customers. The farmer is not out to marry the princess. He wants to impress the woman he's been in love with since they rolled down the hill together at age eight."

"You want to be the fairy godmother that dresses the common man in clothes fit for a king, and helps them to find true love?"

"Why not?" he countered. "Is true love only for the wealthy?"

A strange expression flitted over her eyes. "It's not for the wealthy at all, I'm afraid. They've political alliances and country piles to marry for. I think your intentions are marvelous. *Someone* should be marrying for love. Why not your customers?"

The warmth at her praise was tempered by the strange phrasing of her answer. Had Mrs. Lépine not married for love? Was there some political alliance she'd hoped to make, or country pile she'd wanted to manage?

"What are you working on now?" she asked.

"A new design." He started to pick up the pile of gray superfine, then changed his mind. "I'm waiting for special buttons from the local haberdasher. They were to send a girl round this morning, but as you can see..." He gestured vaguely at the window.

"I *can* see." She stepped closer to the window. "I've never been more envious of anything in my life as I am of the view from your window. Mine is a quarter of this size and only faces a brick wall. It provides dreadful light to paint by."

He remembered glimpsing an easel in her room the first time he'd helped with her dress. She wasn't expecting him to invite her to bring her paints into his workroom, was she? He could not imagine a bigger distraction. The only way to work was *alone*.

"May I see?" She gestured at the superfine.

"It's missing buttons," he reminded her.

"I won't mind if you don't."

He did mind, very much. He never showed anyone unfinished creations. Only once they were perfect and awe-inspiring.

A greatcoat without buttons was not awe-inspiring.

Then again, what did he care about Mrs. Lépine's opinion? Calvin created sophisticated apparel for unsophisticated men with few coins in their pockets. She was the opposite of his intended audience in every way. Besides, once they left this inn, not only would they never see each other again... Their ridiculous contract would prohibit her from disclosing anything she'd glimpsed here. Her thoughts on the matter were absolutely irrelevant.

And yet, when he held up the greatcoat, he could not help but hold his breath.

Her face brightened. "Is it possible to fall in love with a greatcoat? Brummell would. He'd wear that gorgeous coat just as it is, and the next thing you know, all the fashionable gentlemen would strut down Bond Street without buttons. Honestly, I don't know why I haven't heard of your company before."

"We haven't started yet," Calvin admitted. "We've a meeting next week with a potential investor whose faith will make the whole thing possible... or not. When I finish the prototypes, Jonathan will sketch the new costumes. Once we determine the best ones, he'll color them so they look like fashion plates, and the resulting catalogue will be how we sell our creations."

If the snow melted in time for all of that. He grimaced.

"What is it?" she asked.

He shook his head. "Nothing. I'm hurrying to finish my newest design, but one costume more or less won't matter as much as that catalogue. Not only do Jonathan and I need to determine the winning pieces together, he needs time to color the illustrations."

"Maybe he's ahead with his work," she suggested. "If he's anywhere near this snow, perhaps he's painting all the sketches while he's stuck indoors, and you two can determine the best ones later."

"I don't know what he's doing, but it's not that," Calvin said dully. "He sent me the latest sketches a month ago for my review." He flicked his fingers toward the table where they sat.

Mrs. Lépine crept over to the pile of illustrations as though they had fangs that might bite. She stared at the topmost one without touching it, then turned to Calvin so quickly her skirt flared around her ankles.

"I'll do it." Her eyes were overbright.

He frowned. "You'll do what?"

"I'll paint the illustrations." She beamed at him.

He almost laughed at the idea. "Absolutely not. They have to be..."

"*Good?*" she finished, her eyes flashing.

"They must be *perfect*." This was not about her. This was about months of hard work. This was about not squandering what might be his only opportunity to realize a lifelong dream. He stepped protectively next to the illustrations. "These are originals. There are no copies. I cannot risk—"

"I can paint." Her voice cracked. "You would be *lucky* to have me."

He sighed. "Mrs. Lépine..."

"Wait here." She dashed out of the door before he could point out that of course he would wait here, these were his rooms; she was the one trespassing.

He hadn't meant to offend her. Every single detail was of critical importance to the success of this venture. Every aspect, the result of countless hours of careful deliberation and planning.

The name, for instance. *Fit for a Duke*, but not just any duke. Specifically, the Duke of Nottingvale, the popular, handsome bachelor famous for his exclusive Yuletide parties. Men wanted to *be* him. This was his clients' chance.

His manikin had been crafted to Nottingvale's exact proportions. When the duke signed on as primary investor—*if* he signed on—Nottingvale's patronage would be a vital component to how the rest of the country viewed Calvin's designs. It wasn't just the *company's* word that these costumes were fit for a duke. Nottingvale himself would be named on the front page of the catalogue. Calvin's apparel would become famous because Nottingvale was famous.

He would do nothing that might jeopardize the duke's enthusiasm and full cooperation.

Calvin was already nervous enough about meeting the duke in a fortnight. Jonathan had met His Grace before, on multiple occasions, but Jonathan was the sort of man who got on with everyone. Nottingvale had been half sold on the idea from Jonathan's word alone. He'd even had his tailor send his measurements on to Calvin.

This was their opportunity to solidify the partnership. The customers might be rag, tag and bobtail, but the financing for the venture hinged on impressing the Duke of Nottingvale enough for him to part with his money *and* loan his name and likeness.

It was a gamble for everyone.

Nothing could go wrong.

"*Here.*" Mrs. Lépine burst back into the room with a basket and a stack of papers. She shoved the papers at Calvin. "Most of my portraits are at home because I normally paint landscapes, but... Look at the watercolors, not me. This is a Christmas gift for Ursula."

He accepted the stack of papers and glanced down at the first one.

It was Mrs. Lépine and her maid wearing the morning dress and the promenade costume from the January 1814 Ackermann's fashion repository. The resemblance was more than uncanny. Mrs. Lépine had painted them in the same poses as the original fashion plates.

He flipped to the next sheet. Ackermann's, from February. This time, a carriage costume and an evening dress. Next sheet: La Belle Assemblée, March. Then Ackermann's, Assemblée, Ackermann's, Ackermann's, Assemblée.

Mrs. Lépine cleared her throat. "It's—"

"A diary of sorts. A calendar."

"A jest." Her cheeks grew pink. "It's the same gift every year. Us, traipsing through London as the most fashionable duo in history. We didn't really go to all those places dressed like that—"

Calvin hadn't even noticed the backgrounds, but now that she mentioned it, of course these weren't representations of real moments. No woman would wear a riding habit to the theatre, or an opera dress to a picnic. The juxtaposition was on purpose. None of the costumes matched their settings. It was all part of the joke.

"You must think me silly."

"I think you very talented," he admitted as he went through the watercolors a third and then a fourth time.

Jonathan was an exemplary strategist and far more competent than Calvin with pen and ink, but these paintings were brilliant. Mrs. Lépine hadn't *copied* Ackermann's art. She'd *become* it. Wasn't that the very essence of Fit for a Duke?

"Watch." She drew a piece of vellum from her basket and placed it over Jonathan's topmost sketch. The pen lines were barely visible through the semi-transparent paper. "May I?"

His muscles tightened. "That is the only copy—"

"For the moment. Don't worry. No harm will befall your precious original."

She took the sketch and overlaid vellum to the window and pressed it against the glass. The light from the morning sun made the ink lines perfectly visible through the vellum. Her fingers flew over the blank surface with a nub of pencil, deftly copying the original onto the vellum faster than Calvin had thought possible.

When she finished, she handed him the original. He squinted at it from all angles. It was unharmed. There weren't even any indentations from her pencil. He placed it back with the other drawings with great care.

She flopped down onto his sofa and pulled his writing slant onto her lap.

"Normally I would use an easel," she explained, "but vellum is hideous for watercolor, and the colors will run everywhere if the paper is not flat."

She pulled several items from her basket—paper, paints, brushes, jars of water—and dashed at the new sketch for several minutes.

"There," she said with a laugh. "Positively appalling. You must come here to look, because the moment I stand up, everything will run together, as it's already started to do."

He went to look.

It was not one painting but two. Vellum to one side, paper to the right. She was right: the vellum was too wet, but the promise was unmistakable. Just in case he happened to be corkbrained enough to mistake it anyway, she'd painted the same thing on the right, on paper meant for watercolor. It was missing the sharp black delineations of the inked sketch, but the painting itself was breathtaking and vibrant. Anyone who saw such an advertisement would wish to purchase the costume immediately.

"It's dreadful, I know." Her shoulders slumped. "If it were the real sketch, I would have taken my time and done it right. But if you can see the possibilities—"

"*One*," he rasped. "You can paint one, and then I will decide."

He had never decided anything without Jonathan. They were partners; they decided everything together. That was the reason they were meeting the week prior to their appointment with Nottingvale.

But what if there was no week to prepare? What if their best chance at success was sitting in the middle of Calvin's sofa?

He flipped through the sketches until he found the one that he liked the least. An old design, one he and Jonathan had already determined would not be present in the catalogue.

"Here." He held it out. "Paint that."

She took the sketch, then started packing up her basket.

"What are you doing?" he demanded.

She blinked at him in surprise. "Taking this to my easel. These are just my traveling supplies, something I might take with me on a lark. My best paints are in my room."

"And the best light is right here," he reminded her. "Get your paints and your easel. The sketch stays here. None of them leave my sight."

She lit up as if he were magnanimous rather than rude, and dashed off to her room for her easel and paints.

Calvin's stomach fluttered. If she ruined even one of Jonathan's drawings... Then again, if her genius at watercolor could make the illustrations far more impactful than either of them had dared to dream...

It took longer than he expected for her to paint the sketch, given how quickly she'd dashed off her samples, but when at last she showed him the finished work, Calvin's heart tripped and his throat was too tight to speak.

The worst illustration of the lot now looked as though it ought to be on the front cover. It was magnificent. She was a genius. The Duke of Nottingvale would beg to be a full partner, rather than a mere investor. They would all be richer than the Medicis by springtime, and every previously unfashionable man in England would strut about like a peacock in a henhouse.

"All right," he managed. "You can color the illustrations. I suppose you'll be wanting your fifty quid back?"

Her eyes widened. "You would pay *fifty pounds* for my art?"

*Now* she realized what a ridiculous sum of money that was?

"It's my pleasure," she said in a rush, before he could answer. Her eyes were suspiciously glassy, and her words were scratchy. "Just knowing you want my work... It means more to me than you could ever know."

He did not know what to say to that, so he didn't try. He just stood there awkwardly, which was his second-best talent next to designing men's couture.

Mrs. Lépine pointed at the next drawing on the pile. "May I?"

"Please," he said gruffly. "And thank you. Your help will mean more to me than *you* will know."

Oh, God, she was going to cry. Bollocks! Why did he always say the wrong thing?

"Thank you," she said, her voice wobbly. She busied herself with her easel and paints, rather than look at Calvin.

He did the same, pretending to be far more interested in the seam he was sewing than in anything else in the room.

At first, he could scarcely concentrate. There was still the persistent fear that something irrevocable could happen to one of Jonathan's sketches. Even more powerful was the hope, the faith, the belief that this was the missing piece to their puzzle.

Instead of apologetically saying, "Wait until you see the actual costume," they would dazzle their prospective customers with the catalogue alone. People with no intention of purchasing would still subscribe as they did to any fashion repository. Brummell would say something pithy and cutting, which would elevate the costumes all the more. His insult would acknowledge Fit for a Duke; legitimize it. Calvin's fashions would be a topic of conversation at every tea.

He finished the current waistcoat and moved onto the next before he realized how much he was enjoying the companionable silence with Mrs. Lépine. He was constantly *aware* of her presence— it would be difficult to fail to notice a beautiful woman adding paint to his life's work next to the window—but she did not distract him in a negative way. If anything, the weight on his chest was a little lighter. It was surprisingly comforting to know there was someone else in the room, even if they weren't in conversation.

No, not "someone else." He was glad it was *her*. That was why he had been so angry earlier when she'd tried to employ him like a stableboy. He didn't need her fifty quid when the Duke of Nottingvale was poised to invest a thousand pounds. Calvin had wanted Mrs. Lépine to *want* his company. To seek him out for some reason other than the lack of a convenient maid.

And now here she was, lit up by sunlight in his window, the "buttons only" contract tucked away in the shadows of her basket.

She didn't have to be here. She could have left after they had both signed, and instead she had looked for a reason to stay.

After years of preferring solitude, having her in his parlor just felt... right.

Just as it had when he'd held her in his arms.

He didn't realize he was gazing at her mooningly until she peeked around the side of her easel and blushed.

Calvin immediately did the same.

"Sorry," he muttered. "I didn't mean to bother you."

Her eyes held his. "Today is already the pinnacle of my Yuletide."

His stomach chose that moment to announce that it was past noon, and they had been working without cease.

The embarrassing sound should have broken the tension. It did not.

He set down his needle and thread.

Mrs. Lépine set down her paintbrush.

Calvin took a deep breath. She needed him because of her buttons, and he needed her for the illustrations. His next question would determine whether favors were all they had between them, or if there might be the start of something more.

He held her gaze. "Would you like to have luncheon with me?"

She bit her lip. She was going to say no.

He had tried.

"Would you like to have all meals together? Until the snow melts," she added in a rush. "When I come in the morning to button up my gown, I could just... stay with you until it's time to unbutton me."

His mouth dried. There was only one answer to an offer like that.

"Where do I sign?"

# CHAPTER 8

*B*elle glanced over her shoulder and through the large window in what she'd come to think of as her corner of Mr. McAlistair's workroom. The sun was out, and the falling snow had dwindled to the occasional flutter of snowflakes. The storm had passed, or soon would. Before she knew it, the roads would be clear enough for one to drive all the way to Cressmouth.

She had never wanted anything less.

The past four days had been a delight. Racing next door first thing every morning, where Mr. McAlistair would greet her with a smile that melted her knees. Then they'd button up her dress and get to work. Work! She, Lady Isabelle, had *work*.

It was her, not "Mr. Brough," who Mr. McAlistair trusted to paint his business partner's sketches. Oh, very well, "Mrs. Lépine" was still a pseudonym, but at least Belle hadn't needed to pretend to be a man to be taken seriously.

She was doing work that *mattered*, work that would mean something, work that could bring hope and new possibilities to countless people. Her efforts here today might one day be in people's homes, be the topic of conversation at dinner, or be marked with a bit of ribbon as a potential customer decided which of his favorites he might purchase.

It wasn't *exactly* the same as publishing original art under her own name, but it was an honor and a privilege to be chosen and trusted with something so important and irreplaceable.

Mostly trusted, she amended, with a subtle glance at Mr. McAlistair. Belle had mastered the art of sliding her eyes just above or beside her easel in order to gaze at him without it looking as though her focus had broken at all.

He trusted her enough that he no longer flinched whenever she selected a new sketch, but he could not hide his almost comical relief every time she presented him with a completed illustration and he discovered it was actually good and not ruined.

Not "good," Belle reminded herself. He needed these to be *perfect*. Mr. McAlistair demanded no less than perfection from himself.

He needn't worry.

She could barely concentrate on her easel because she kept staring in awe at him.

He was fearlessly creative, cutting and sewing and discarding in order to cut and sew again and again. Slight variations, dramatic variations, wildly different combinations. Nothing was sacred until it completed some vision that he had to create with his hands and see before him to know it was right. Only then did a slight smile tease the edge of his lips.

His work took one hundred percent of his attention. She suspected a dragon could fly up and breathe fire at the windowpane and he wouldn't notice. It was as though nothing existed but him and his designs.

Until he laid down his completed greatcoat and lifted his gaze to hers.

She jerked her eyes back to her easel, but it was too late. He had caught her watching him. Her cheeks burned. She pretended none of that had occurred and that she had been deeply engrossed in her illustration the entire time.

Only half the sketches had been painted. Belle wanted to complete the rest not just to prove herself competent and useful, but because the project was exciting, and Mr. McAlistair was incredible. Working with someone was a new experience in general, but working with *him* was better than anything she might have dreamt.

She wouldn't be there when he and his partner pored through the finished watercolors to determine which finalists would be accepted into the catalogue, but she had no doubt any investor worth his salt would be just as impressed as she was. She might not be present for the making of the catalogue, but she'd see it everywhere once it became the talk of the town.

"How is the new illustration coming along?"

came Mr. McAlistair's seductive rumble from just a few feet away.

"Er...fine," she said. Or sort of said. Words tended to tangle in her throat whenever he was close enough to smell, to touch.

As if it wasn't pressure enough to know how critical it was for every sweep of her brush to be perfect, for *Belle* to be perfect. He was putting so much faith and trust in her. She had to deserve it.

"There." She stepped back from her easel. "You can look if you like."

Of course he could look if he liked. The illustrations were his property. She was helping, but he didn't *need* her. He and his partner would get on just fine without her as soon as the snow melted. And Belle would go back to painting everyday scenes for a book she would never publish.

Mr. McAlistair joined her before the easel, his body close enough for her to feel his heat and breathe in his masculine scent.

Perhaps that was why she babbled, "The outfit is a delight, but where is this supposed to be? There are—" She counted quickly. "—nine drummers drumming in the background. Is it supposed to be some sort of parade?"

He shrugged. "According to Jonathan, adverts needn't portray *realistic* circumstances to be effective. Besides, don't forget I've had a peek at your calendar. Were any of those settings practical?"

"Very practical," she assured him. "I would never ride bareback on a stallion without a satin opera gown and a shell lace tippet."

He grinned at her. "You should sell your visions back to Ackermann."

Her heart thumped. He was teasing, she reminded herself. Ackermann would never purchase its own designs, which meant Mr. McAlistair wasn't really saying he thought her art was good enough to be sold or used commercially.

"Or paint something else," he suggested. "And then you can sell it to the world."

Oh.

He really *was* saying her art was commercially viable.

Her heart beat so fast, it felt as though it was taking flight.

His bright brown eyes held hers in their thrall. "May I see the rest of your paintings? As lovely as your Christmas gift to your maid is, I'm certain you must have more art next door that I haven't seen."

"N-no," she stammered. "That is, yes, I do have a few pieces, but I'm not ready... for..."

She trailed off and clamped her lips together before she spilled all her secrets.

Ursula wasn't the only one who would receive original Lady Isabelle artwork this Yuletide. When Belle wasn't working side by side with Mr. McAlistair, she hunched over the floor in her cramped guestroom, painting a series of candid watercolors of Mr. McAlistair working on his designs. Cutting, sewing, measuring, outfitting his manikin.

The series would not be suitable for inclusion into his catalogue, but she hoped it would bring him good memories of the work he'd put into his dream... and the short time he and Belle had spent together.

"That's all right," he said. "I understand. I've never shown anyone my unfinished work or the designs I decided not to pursue." When his gaze flicked to his manikin, and his eyes crinkled. "Well, until you, of course."

"This week has been full of first times for me, as well," she admitted. She ran her finger along the wooden rim of the easel. "Other than Ursula, no one sees my work at all."

He tilted his head. "How is she?"

"Better every day, they tell me, although I haven't been allowed to see her."

Not being *allowed* something she wanted was another first. Oh, to be sure, Belle's family laid down laws and tugged the reins. But outside of her home, no one would dare naysay Lady Isabelle.

Mrs. Lépine, on the other hand...

"I'm glad to hear she's improving. Where did you say you were off to once the snow clears?"

She hadn't said. Every time he asked something personal, no matter how innocent or insignificant, she'd deflected the question rather than risk accidentally giving a clue to her real identity.

But she was tired of being unable to share any part of her true self with the man she was spending every day with. The better she came to know Mr. McAlistair, the more she liked him. She wished he could know her, too, if only superficially.

"I'm visiting friends and family for Christmastide," she said.

There. That was true, if not special or unique. She imagined every guest in the posting house shared the same festive agenda. Many were doubtlessly en route to Marlowe Castle for the Yuletide season. They might even attend some of the same assemblies or theatre productions, although with the influx of tourists making the annual pilgrimage to Cressmouth, running into anyone specific would be unlikely.

"I'm sorry the snow has spoilt your plans." The light from the window gave his hair a celestial glow. She longed to paint him, just like this. "Your friends and family must miss you."

Angelica would, yes. But Belle was not expected at her brother's cottage for another week. She doubted Vale had left London yet.

"Come to think of it," she said with a little laugh, "I'm uncertain my brother expects me at all."

His brows shot skyward. "Why wouldn't he?"

"My brother..." *is the Duke of Nottingvale.* "...is too busy to plan his own soirées. I used to help."

Not "help." Belle used to do absolutely everything. Mother believed running Vale's various households would foster necessary skills and increase Belle's attractiveness to potential titled suitors. Over the years, she had learned every detail and could have run a dozen households in her sleep. That was, if there'd been any time to sleep. Or to paint. Or to breathe.

No one was more shocked than Belle when

she'd finally rebelled. All of these demands weren't her duty at all. She was *not* a wife, these were *not* her households, and this was *not* her cross to bear. There was no time to just be Belle.

So, she'd stopped helping with the Christmas parties. A minor insubordination, perhaps, but the first time she'd attempted to assert her independence to her mother.

Mother's response, of course, was to say that Belle was not now nor would ever be independent. She was obliged to do as she was told, first by her family, and then by her husband. The sooner she resigned herself to the facts of life, the sooner they could all have done with this silly tantrum.

Vale had been the one to come to Belle's rescue. He was horrified to realize how many responsibilities his little sister had undertaken, and declared at once that she was not obliged to exhaust herself like a maid-of-all-work when the dukedom's coffers had more than enough coin to employ additional staff to handle any duty.

So, Belle had got her way. She wasn't in charge of anything anymore. No longer needed, wanted, noticed. No longer significant in the least. Hurrah.

Winning had been worse than losing.

"I haven't any siblings," Mr. McAlistair said, and leaned one shoulder beside the window. "Does that make me advantaged or disadvantaged?"

"Both," she answered without hesitation, and chuckled at his confusion. She tried to explain. "I love my brother more than anything. He loves me, too. I have never doubted it. But he was born the important one, whilst I was born expendable."

She'd spent a lifetime trying to prove herself otherwise, but longed to do it on her own terms. To be important because she was Belle, rather than because she served some easily replaceable purpose.

"Surely not *expendable*," Mr. McAlistair said in horror.

"They would never harm me," Belle assured him. "They just don't... see me."

No one did.

To the beau monde, she was the Duke of Nottingvale's sister, rather than her own person. To her mother, she was a little doll to be posed and placed wherever her mother saw fit.

Belle wasn't supposed to have thoughts in her pretty head. She couldn't even color theatre bills without doing so under an assumed name. Lady Isabelle had plenty of money. Why play at some laughable post to earn a pittance? She should go shopping instead. Perhaps the right ribbon in her bonnet would help her attract the right man.

According to Mother, the right man was someone like the Earl of Lunsford or the Duke of Westlington, both of whom had deep coffers, enormous estates, and thrice as many years as Belle. They were old enough to be her grandfather. Not that a wife need be attracted to her husband. No one wed because they *liked* each other. They married to cement their dynasty. Didn't she *want* to be a rich, powerful duchess?

No, actually. Belle did not. She would do it, of

course, because it was her duty to do so, and she'd already disappointed her family enough by dragging her feet for this long. Besides, what else could she do? Her place was in Society. It was the only world she knew, the only place she was of value.

Mother was right: Belle *had* learnt all the skills. No one would laugh to hear Lady Isabelle was the Countess of Lunsford, the way the publishing houses and traveling circuses had sniggered when she had tried to show them her art. She belonged in the beau monde. Accepting her destiny was nothing more than changing which shadow she lived under.

Her husband's name would always be far more important than hers.

"How about you?" She put down her brushes. "You've the presentation, of course, and then what?"

"Seasonal festivities," he said in a tone that sounded anything but jolly. "If the presentation goes well, I won't want to do anything but work on plans for the company. Waiting until after Twelfth Night will be torture."

"Your presentation will go splendidly," she assured him. "Your investors will be more excited about your couture than they will be for Christmas."

Thanks to their contract, Belle would not be able to squeal, *I know him!* when his fashions became the talk of London. Mr. McAlistair's name would be as well-known as the Duke of Nottingvale's or Beau Brummell's.

As for Belle's name, well... perhaps a pseudonym wasn't the worst that could befall her. It gave her the freedom to be here with Mr. McAlistair. To paint, and to be taken seriously as an artist. She could throw herself into his arms for that alone. He *saw* her. He liked her; he appreciated her. He made her wish she could feel like this every day.

"Tea?" he asked, pushing away from the window.

She nodded. "Please."

The sun was beginning to set, which brought them to Belle's second favorite part of the day: *not* working together. Mr. McAlistair would make tea, and they would sit side by side before his great window and watch the sun slowly sink behind the rolling snow-covered hills, bathing them with a pink and orange watercolor of its own.

He placed a steaming cup of tea into her hand and joined her on the cushion. He was close enough that she could have laid her head on his shoulder if she wanted to. She did want to. She wanted to nestle into him and have him tuck his arm about her and watch the sunset wrapped in each other's arms as their tea grew cold, forgotten.

When he thought her attention was elsewhere, Mr. McAlistair looked at her like he wanted those things, too. He gazed at her as though the only thing stopping him from reaching for her was the boiling liquid clutched in his hand, which was the real reason for mucking about with tea. He wasn't thirsty, or at least not for that. He looked at her as though he were hungry for *her*.

Until she accidentally met his eyes, of course.

And then they immediately cast their gazes out of the window, their words tripping over each other to be the first to make some inane comment about evergreens or holly.

She should be glad he wasn't as rakish as he dressed, she reminded herself. She was a lady, soon to be betrothed to some lord. Under no circumstances should she embroil herself in a torrid affair with a devastatingly handsome tailor.

All it would take was one kiss, and she would forget her station completely.

She must stay very, very vigilant.

"Thank you," he said softly. "For helping."

*Thank* you *for disrobing me* seemed an inappropriate response, so Belle simply gave a quick nod behind her teacup. "It's my pleasure."

Why had she mentioned pleasure? The moment the word was out of her mouth, his gaze dropped to her lips. Her skin heated and tingled in awareness.

His eyes met hers. "You are astoundingly talented, Mrs. Lépine."

Oh, there it was. A beautiful compliment spoilt by her dreadful pseudonym. She had never impressed anyone before, and hated that she could only do so from behind a false name. She wished, just for once, just with *him*, that she could still be impressive as herself.

But he could never find out. No one could. Her reputation would be worse than ruined. She'd not only lose her place in Society and her good favor with her mother, she'd tarnish her entire family's name in the process.

That was why his idea to sign a contract had been brilliant. She would ensure he never learnt her true identity, but even if he did, he could not disclose it. No matter what, they would go their separate ways, and that would be that.

Belle would be temporary, their stolen moments together a secret, just like she wanted.

Like they both wanted.

And if a tiny part of her wanted nothing of the sort, well, that was because every time Belle thought, she thought all the wrong things. Thoughts like, *I wish this was real*. Or, *if it's to remain secret anyway, what's the harm in one little kiss?* Thoughts like, *I want more*.

She couldn't help it. He was genuine and honest. He was a creative genius who appreciated and encouraged her contributions. He was happy to act as a team. He was proud of the work they did together. He smelt of sandalwood and sunshine, and sent her heated sidelong glances that could melt a woman's stays right off her body... that was, if Belle were wearing any.

He touched the side of her face and lowered his mouth toward hers. "Stop me."

She pressed her lips to his.

Stop him? Nothing could stop this. Their kiss had been inevitable for days, building up power with every stolen glance and unfastened button until they could not be in the same room without the constant awareness of each other heating the air.

A chaste kiss was all it could be, something fast

and passionless to prove their attraction to be nothing but folly.

Except the kiss wasn't chaste and perfunctory, but demanding, hot, open-mouthed. Her arms were about his neck, her hands in his hair. Her bosom pressed tight against his chest, unfettered by whalebone stays or rules about what she should and should not do when alone in the room of a handsome gentleman.

No, not "gentleman." But this lack of status didn't feel like a lack at all. It felt like a reprieve. A benediction. He did not feel like a mistake. He tasted like the answer to a prayer.

So what if he couldn't keep her, if she couldn't keep him? This kiss wasn't about forever. It was about today, tonight, the sunset bathing their features as they pulled each other into a deeper embrace.

This kiss was about searing him into her memory, even though she could not invite him into her life. Especially because of that, she wanted to remember every moment, every brush of his lips, every touch of his hand, every contour of his hard, warm frame pressing against her soft curves.

When she closed her eyes tonight, she wanted to remember the taste of his kiss, the heat of his skin, the way she longed to breathe in deeply whenever he was near in order to fill her lungs with his scent and carry part of him inside her, if only for a second.

It was more than just a kiss. She was *happy* when she was with him. She felt like herself, like she'd found a home here in his arms. She hoped the snow fell for decades so she could stay nestled in his embrace and never have to leave. She wanted—

"I'm sorry," he gasped, pulling his mouth from hers as though the separation caused him as much pain as it did her. "Forgive me."

There it was. An end to the memory.

"Don't apologize." She forced herself to meet his eyes. "I've been wanting it too, even if I should not have."

"You're right. We should not have." His voice was firm with resolve. "I shan't let it happen again."

"Nor I," she agreed, a mere breath before their mouths found each other again.

How was she supposed to stay away from him, from *this?* Was it even necessary to try? No one would ever know she'd allowed her mouth to be plundered with kisses. No one but Belle, who would think of him every night as she crawled into bed and wished he were there beside her.

But it could never be more than kisses.

This time, when he lifted his mouth from hers, he did not pull fully away. "Mrs. Lépine—"

"Belle," she whispered.

She could not be Lady Isabelle with him, but nor could she remain Mrs. Lépine. Both felt a lie. When they kissed, she wanted him to be kissing *her.*

"Belle," he repeated, his voice soft. "I'm Calvin. Will you be back tomorrow?"

"I'll be back for as long as you want me."

"Ah," he growled, as though she had just tempted a tiger. "I'll always want you."

She turned her back so that he could not see how his words affected her and lifted her hair from her nape. "Would you..."

"It would be my pleasure."

Every new button unfastened felt like another part of her soul coming loose. She could not allow her desires to rein free. When he finished, she turned around, clutching her bodice to her chest.

"Just kisses," she informed him.

He nodded. "Just kisses."

But already, she wanted more.

# CHAPTER 9

*C*alvin's heart skipped when the knock sounded against his door. He leapt to his feet and bolted across the room to answer without delay.

Was it less than a fortnight ago when he had hated even the slightest interruption to his work? It felt like a different life. Belle was no interruption. She was the reason for the excited flutter in his stomach. Besides, Calvin had not been working. Could he remember a time when he had ever not been working?

He flung open the door and smiled as though it had been two years since last he'd seen her, rather than two interminable hours.

Her hazel eyes sparkled up at him. "Your room smells like chestnuts."

"That's because I'm roasting chestnuts." He cocked an eyebrow. "Would you like some?"

"Hmm." She touched a finger to the edge of his lapel. "You might have something I'd like."

He pulled her into his arms and kissed her,

swinging her into his guest chamber so he could kick the door closed with the heel of his leather shoe. The room smelt of chestnuts, but she smelt of soap and freshly washed hair, a combination that now haunted his dreams.

When he rang for his baths, he thought only of her. Whenever he unbuttoned her gown so she could slip back to her chamber before her bath arrived, he would sink back onto his sofa with his eyes closed tight and his face toward their shared wall, imagining he could feel the heat of the steamy water and the slippery softness of her soapy skin.

Just kisses, she had said, and of course she was right. Or maybe wrong. Her kisses were the reason he woke up every morning, and her kisses were also what would destroy him when they departed their separate ways.

He could not think of that, could not allow himself to imagine how the future would feel. If a simple wall the width of a man's hand was an untenable barrier, how then was he meant to withstand miles between them, years dividing them, a lifetime of never meeting again?

Just kisses. Just kisses. He would repeat it to himself until it was true, until it was the only thing he wanted and the only thing that mattered.

Once the snow stopped, so too would this interlude. He would not be sad, but rather sated. He would have gorged himself on so many kisses that he would be positively drunk with them when he stumbled from the posting house and into the sunlight.

Like a drunkard's thoughts, those wonderful memories would blur and fade, and before long, he wouldn't even notice the miles and years between them. It would be a dream they had once shared together. A fine memory of a certain time and place. A bit of lace, sewn into his soul. Just a few kisses, nothing more.

He pulled his mouth away and pretended he had no difficulty breathing at all when he asked, "Chestnut?" as though there had been no interruption in their conversation. There hadn't been.

Kisses could never interrupt. Kisses were the conversation.

She touched her fingertips to her lips as though she could still feel his kiss there and nodded faintly. "Yes, please."

Belle held a leather portfolio in one hand, but drew no attention to it. Perhaps she was still deciding whether she was ready to show him whatever she carried inside. In the meantime, the least he could do was offer her a toasted treat.

He'd placed both chairs closer to the fireplace in anticipation of her visit, and now he offered her the more comfortable of the two. Had he known he would entertain a beautiful woman in his guest chamber, he would have packed more than one teacup and saucer, and a large pan for roasting chestnuts, rather than this small one that barely toasted enough for Calvin to snack on when he was alone.

They would simply have to be here all night, if that was what was necessary. Side by side before the fire, roasting small batches of chestnuts one handful at a time, letting them cool slightly before attempting to open the cracked shells in order to savor the hot, sweet morsels inside.

Belle grinned at him as she kicked off her slippers and curled into the chair, the tips of her stockinged toes peeking flirtatiously from beneath the flouncy vandyke hem of her gown.

Calvin had the fleeting thought that he would miss moments like this just as much as the kisses, but he pushed this aside and concentrated on his task by the fire. This was a holiday for both of them. A holiday from real life, to which they would both return soon enough. No sense allowing nettlesome reality to ruin the moment any sooner than necessary.

"Do you always pack chestnuts in your valise?" she teased.

"Not at all," he informed her. "I pack *dishes* in my valise, and order a delivery of chestnuts once I reach my destination."

Her eyes widened. "Was *that* what was in the parcel that first night?" She burst out laughing. "I should not have taken so long to work up the courage to knock."

"That was your first night, not mine," he reminded her, "so no, by then I had already received my order of chestnuts." Technically, by then he had already received his second order of chestnuts. Had he but known there would be reason to ration them... "The parcel you saw was of blue superfine. I am still waiting on those special buttons."

She accepted the teacup full of chestnuts. "Well, at least you got the important bit."

He was inclined to agree, which was yet another surprise in a week of surprises. If the buttons had arrived but not the chestnuts, his final prototype would be finished, and he and Belle wouldn't be having this cozy moment at all.

It was strange to think that all the things he had long preferred to do in solitude were even better enjoyed with Belle at his side.

"I admit," she said, after licking her finger, "I hope the buttons arrive before I leave, because I am desperate to see the final costume completed. Every design you've shown me has impressed me even more than the last, so do not be surprised if I swoon into your manly embrace upon seeing it."

"Everyone does," he assured her. "I owe all of my musculature to the drudgery of endlessly catching those who swoon into my arms."

If only it were so easy! Having the Duke of Nottingvale keel over in a dead faint from excessive exposure to high-end fashion would be the best of all outcomes.

He tried not to think about the worst. If the presentation went poorly, if Nottingvale rescinded his name and his likeness, or declined to invest in the project, there would be no second chance, no *Ah, well, I suppose we must settle for some other young handsome duke willing to wager a good portion of his wealth on an unprecedented catalogue scheme directed at the population with the least fashion sense or extra coins for frivolous shopping.*

Coming this far had been a fluke of good fortune and Calvin knew it. There would be no second chance. Not for him, not for Jonathan, and not for their grand idea. He *had* to make it work.

"Oh! I've been wondering." Belle lowered her cup of chestnuts. "Do you have a name for your collection of couture?"

Calvin hesitated. No one but Jonathan MacLean and the Duke of Nottingvale knew any details about the secret project. The idea was to keep the cards to their collective chests and make a splash all at once.

But Belle wasn't just anyone. She was the talented artist who painted the illustrations he and Jonathan would use in the presentation. At this point, she'd already seen all of the designs. She felt as though she were part of the team.

"'Fit for a Duke,'" said Calvin, adopting a sophisticated accent and facial expression. "'Finished tailoring available for rent or purchase.'"

"Fit for a *Duke?*" she repeated. "A peer would never wear garments that aren't bespoke."

"That is why peers are not the audience," he pointed out. "Non-aristocrats dream of being *like* aristocrats. Besides, 'Fit for Common Man' doesn't have the same ring to it, does it?"

"True," she said, "and clever. You're right. Everyone aspires to rise to a higher social level, no matter where one finds oneself on the ladder."

"I don't. I like being an unknown tailor. It's my costumes that I hope will become famous. The public deserves them."

"And what do you deserve? Should you not gain recognition for your efforts in addition to financial compensation and the joy of sharing your work?"

He shrugged. "I don't care what people think about *me*. I'm trying to improve how they see each other. I want to give them the means to feel confident and fashionable, even if they're spending the evening at home with a book and a cat."

Her brow furrowed. "You really wouldn't wish to be a duke, if titles could be had for the mere wanting?"

"I don't want to be anywhere near the beau monde," he said with feeling. "Clothing aristocrats is the closest I'd ever wish to come. I enjoy dressing the part, but being forced to live it would be a nightmare."

She made a face, but voiced no comment.

"Has waking up *bon ton* always been a favorite dream of yours?" he asked.

"No," she said. "It hasn't been that."

He was happier than he had a right to be that she didn't dream of becoming a lady. It was not something he could give her. Not something he could even pretend to want. He was awkward around others even when they didn't expect much of him. Having to meet High Society standards would be impossible. A ballroom? He shuddered to think.

For months, he'd been dreading this journey to Cressmouth, whose pre-Yule population was lower than Vauxhall Gardens on a warm summer day. Cressmouth was not London, a fact which was very much in its favor. But during the festive season, the village nonetheless ballooned in size to accommodate visitors from all over England, from the common folk whom Calvin wished to clothe to Peers of the Realm, who barely acknowledged the existence of common folk like Calvin.

At least all he had to survive was a single Christmastide, and then he could return to the safety and comfort of his ordinary world.

Well, not the *same* world as before. If all went well, his new world would revolve around the implementation and launch of an exciting new business venture.

And if *that* went well... If the new company were popular and profitable and stable... Calvin would finally be able to consider making a few more changes to his world.

Belle caught his gaze and blushed. "You're wondering what's in my leather case."

He had been thinking of something else entirely, but he was willing to take whatever she wished to share.

"All right." She took a deep breath. "I'll show you."

She set her now empty teacup aside and pulled the portfolio onto her lap. It looked expensive and new, as though she had purchased it only that morning and was just now opening it for the first time.

Inside was a thick stack of watercolors that didn't look new at all. Some of the papers were crisp, whilst the edges of others had softened with age.

She hesitated for a long moment, then shoved the whole onto Calvin's lap without meeting his eyes. "These are less fanciful than the ones for Ursula."

That was not the only difference. While the other paintings had been whimsical juxtapositions of the latest couture in all the wrong settings, these watercolors seemed to have nothing to do with London or fashion. It was as though Belle had painted bucolic winter scenes by glancing out from a high window and painting whatever she happened to spy.

The first was several girls giggling to themselves as they hung mistletoe throughout a parlor. Next was a snowball fight, then the staff of a large kitchen making Christmas pudding, then children of all ages sledding down a steep hill, then hundreds of people in woolen caps and bright mittens huddled in an amphitheatre as a play unfolded before them. There was a row of red sleighs filled with jolly patrons, being pulled along by white horses. Here was an assembly of some sort, filled with musicians and grand ball gowns, with sprigs of holly tucked behind every lady's ear. And here were dozens of friends wassailing, some with serious expressions and others crumpled against each other with laughter as though they could no longer recall the words to the carols and had given up trying to make sense.

"These are incredible," he murmured as he went through each one in turn.

It was as though rather than painting a landscape or a still life, she had captured a specific moment in time. The lurch in one's stomach as the sled started down the hill, the fragrant aroma of nutmeg and cinnamon when a wooden handle stirred the pudding, the joyful mischievousness of planting mistletoe exactly where one's unsuspecting future beau was bound to pass. It felt as though he were peering into the lives of real people.

In fact... He returned to the first painting and went through them again, this time more slowly. These *were* real people. Or at least one real person. In the background of each merry scene was a very familiar face: Belle, watching from this corner or that with a wistful half-smile on her face.

This was the real reason she hadn't wanted him to see her art, he realized. Not because she believed it to be unskilled, but because she had painted herself into the fun, carefree moments of other people's lives. Not as a sister hanging holly, but a distant shadow in the background. Always present, but never part. Dressed impeccably, hands gloved and folded, invisible to the people whose joy she watched with such longing... and likely just as unseen by the average person who paged through these paintings, too entranced by the colorful cheer in the foreground to notice a still, silent presence almost too far out of focus to register.

"I painted these for a Yuletide collection," she explained haltingly. "A book containing all the times... I wouldn't really publish such nonsense," she added in haste, her fingers twisting. "It was just a lark; a way to pass the time. Here, I'll put them back into the portfolio."

"Of course you should publish your art. It's

joyful and exquisite." He gave her a crooked smile. "And next time, consider riding a sled rather than watching from behind an evergreen."

Her cheeks flushed scarlet. "I could never. My mother would disown me for even considering it. And if riding a sled is out of the question, publishing my little illustrations..."

"Your illustrations are breathtaking," he told her firmly. He was glad he was in no danger of meeting her family. They sounded judgmental and impossible to please. If someone as perfect as Belle wasn't good enough, Calvin would be the worst disappointment they'd ever seen. "Sledding might be dangerous, but I don't see what harm a book could bring. If it were truly a problem, I suppose one could consider a pseudonym."

She flinched as if dodging a blow. "Pseudonyms can be just as dreadful as gossip." She stuffed the watercolors back into the portfolio and closed it tight, as if erasing them from existence. "It is better to give no impression at all than to make a bad one."

He happened to agree, although he did not think Belle was in any danger of making a poor impression. Calvin, on the other hand, never knew what to say. He dressed as he did so that his dashing clothes would speak for him and he needn't cock things up pretending to act on top of it. Making a good impression without having to say a word was the raison d'être of Fit for a Duke.

Which was what he should concentrate on, he reminded himself sternly as he added a few more chestnuts to the pan over the fire. There was a very good reason he had vowed not to complicate his life until after his company became a success. The next few weeks would be difficult enough without adding a beautiful distraction to the mix. Once the company was a success, he would be able to consider matters of the heart.

But first, he needed to finish his prototypes and prepare the materials for his presentation. Then, he would spend days with Jonathan to discuss their plans before they met with Nottingvale and attempted to woo him of every spare penny. Next came the worst part: he and Jonathan were then expected to remain at Nottingvale's cottage as honored guests for all twelve days of Christmas.

There would be no time to think of Belle at all.

# CHAPTER 10

The following afternoon, Calvin could not stop watching Belle paint from the corner of his eye. Although she was illustrating the sole copies of sketches that would determine the Duke of Nottingvale's potential enthusiasm as an investor, Calvin was no longer certain if the strange flutters in his belly were from nerves... or for Belle.

Working together wasn't just one of his favorite parts of the day. It felt right; it felt normal. It felt like doing anything else would be a grievous mistake. Belle's presence made everything better. Not just passionate embraces or mundane tasks like work, but simple moments like spreading soft butter on fresh bread, or silly moments like laying on their backs beside the window to point out fantastical shapes in the clouds.

He no longer liked the idea that she knocked on his door due to any external obligation. Jonathan's sketches, which had once seemed too numerous to count, were within a day or two of all being painted. And Calvin was within a day or two of finishing the gown he'd been secretly designing for Belle. One that she could fasten and unfasten on her own, so that her daily visits would not be because she needed his help, but because she wanted *him*.

Making the perfect gown had proved impossible, which for Calvin was an unfamiliar and unwelcome situation. Although he'd switched from ladies' fashions to men's apparel over a decade ago, his talent as a designer was not the problem. Lack of source material was. If he did not have the proper buttons to finish his final prototype for Fit for a Duke, he certainly did not have the silks and gauze and accoutrements fit for a woman like Belle.

Yet he was determined to create the most dazzling fashion he could from whatever he had. He didn't want her to wear his design as a last resort, but because she looked resplendent.

Belle glanced over her shoulder toward the window. "That's almost the last of the light. I'll move my easel."

His heart leapt. "I'll get the sofa."

He looked forward to sunset the way a sapling looked forward to spring. Twilight made the constant awareness between them blossom into something more.

With all traces of work gone, and the sofa arranged before the window just so, she nestled into his embrace as if his arms had been designed to hold her close. He felt as though every part of him had been made to bring her every pleasure he could.

Tonight's kiss was as sweet and as dangerous as all the others. The beguiling nectar of forbidden promises that could not be made and the temptation to surrender anyway.

He could no longer fool himself into thinking his life would return to normal once he left Houville behind. He had not been lonely before because his solitude had been by choice. His heart would now make a far different choice, if living forever in the fantasy world of a snowbound posting house were possible.

But the snow would soon leave, and so would they, each riding off their separate ways. A rash, foolish part of him wanted to beg her to join him at the Yuletide party, but of course it was not in his power to issue invitations to someone else's household, much less a peer of the realm Calvin desperately needed to impress.

Besides, he wouldn't put Belle through that. Calvin had never met a lord in any capacity other than a paid provider of services, and doubted a fortnight in the duke's company would bring much Christmas cheer. More importantly, the ducal residence would be nothing like the Hoot & Holly. There would be no adjoining rooms, no languorous snuggles to watch the sunset, no unbuttoning of gowns between heated kisses.

The best plan, the only reasonable plan, was to put his full concentration into securing the Duke of Nottingvale's full cooperation and investment, so that Calvin might soon be in a position where he could offer Belle something better than a temporary stay beneath someone else's roof.

"What are you thinking about?" she asked.

"Fit for a Duke," he replied. It was not untrue, but nor was the successful launch of his company the only dream he wanted to come true now.

"How did you become such a skilled tailor?"

"Trial and error, I suppose, as well as indefatigable stubbornness," he said wryly. "My mother was an in-demand modiste to peeresses and other influential ladies of the ton. She was very talented, and did not require the help of a lad in short pants. I was determined to contribute anyway."

Belle smiled against his chest. "I don't imagine fashionable ladies wished to have a little boy cut their gowns."

"They did not," he confirmed. "Because of the wealth of my mother's clientele, we were not hurting for money. I was left to my own devices, and allowed to do as I pleased. What I pleased, it turned out, was to rescue every thread and remnant from my mother's scrap bin in order to fashion creations of my own."

"And you discovered you were brilliant?"

"I discovered I didn't have the least idea what I was doing," he said with a laugh. "Good design was not something I could replicate just by looking at it, at least not back then."

"Did your mother teach you?"

"One of her assistants took pity on me, and answered my endless questions when she broke for her noon meal. How to do this kind of stitch or that, and how to know which one to choose.

Which cuts were for which fabrics, how much they cost, and how much they might be sold for. The logic of prices meant nothing to me, as I could neither make purchases nor sales, but at last my continued interest reached my mother's ears."

"What did she do?"

"She took one look at the rags I'd cobbled together and burst out laughing. I was humiliated. But then she gave me all of her old fashion repositories. Mother subscribed to them all, and even commissioned unique designs straight from Paris. It was a university education in two cedar chests."

"You were in heaven?"

"Or in a fever. I started at the beginning, recreating every design in every collection using the material I had at hand, until I knew each cut and seam by heart. Mother's assistants would take turns as my model. I practiced sewing to their sizes without touching them or measuring, until I could fathom anyone's dimensions with a cursory glance."

Her eyes widened. "Can you still?"

"That's how I fashioned Duke." As well as the gown he was making for Belle.

"What did you do with all the clothes you were making?"

"Took them apart in order to reuse the material in something else. Until the day one of my mother's assistants asked if she could keep the dress that I had made to match her figure. It was hopelessly unfashionable. Mother didn't relinquish her fashion plates until they were out of season, and my reuse of material meant my gowns had extra seams from combining disparate pieces together."

"But if the assistant wanted to keep it... she must have felt it looked well on her?"

"She could have passed for a client," he admitted with pride. "The extra seams were well hidden, and I'd taken enough liberties with the original design that on first glance Mother thought Poppy was clothed in couture so new it hadn't yet reached London."

Belle laughed in delight. "What did she do when she found out?"

He grinned. "Poppy kept the gown, and I was allowed to work with new fabric instead of old. By the time I was an adolescent, I was the one designing the gowns from my private workroom down the corridor. Everyone thought it was my mother's doing—she could scarcely admit her fashions came from her child, rather than from Paris—and soon we were busier than ever."

"Your mother's shop." Belle's head jerked back. "Where was it located?"

"You wouldn't know it," he assured her.

His mother had become just as pretentious as her customers with age, and only worked with the crème de la crème of the bon ton. Besides, Belle would have been an adolescent herself around the time Calvin's mother fell ill.

"She died twelve years ago last autumn," he explained. He still carried the loss with him.

Belle's expression indicated she was no stranger to loss herself. That was the danger of loving someone. There was no guarantee you would get to keep them.

He glanced away. "Technically, I inherited Mother's business. But when she passed, her customers went elsewhere, too. Modistes are women. Tailors are men. Learning an entirely new sphere of fashion gave me something constructive to do besides grieve. Once I became competent, it didn't take long to innovate."

"Did you make just as big a splash as before?"

"No splash at all," he said dryly. "I contacted the male halves of my mother's prior customers, but of course lords already had their own preferred tailors. There was no hope of a twenty-year-old lad supplanting already famous tailors to the elite. Then I realized I didn't want to replace them. The vast majority of our country's men has no coronet, but still seeks to look their best and impress their future wives. Why not help them?"

"Money, I suppose," she murmured.

He nodded. "Tutors and blacksmiths cannot pay the same prices as an earl, but there are far more tutors and blacksmiths than earls. Not to mention an entirely new class that seems to be forming. The changes in the textile industry, for example, has put money into the pockets of people who never had it before. High Society might consider these upwardly ambitious tadpoles their social inferiors, but they are often the wealthiest of their villages or parishes and hunger to look presentable as well."

"Not to look presentable," she corrected slowly. "To wear items fit for a duke."

"Precisely. They don't have the knowledge or the connections of the beau monde, but soon, they won't need them. The perfect costume will be sent post-haste." His cheeks heated. "I cannot imagine what my mother would think of such a venture."

Belle's eyes filled with warmth. "She would be so proud of her son."

Would she? His heart knocked hollowly against his chest. Losing his mother so young was the tragedy that never ceased hurting. He wasn't just her son. They'd been cohorts, two fashion-mad knights of the needle charging after the same shared dream. Beginning anew without her had been miserable.

It had taught him how dangerous it was to allow someone close, because they could leave at any time and take a part of you with them.

If he was already afraid of how empty his world would seem without Belle in it after a mere fortnight of her company, it would be infinitely worse to allow their connection to bloom into something deeper, only to be plucked apart by fate. As much as he longed to pursue her in the future, a successful company was no guarantee of winning a woman's heart—and hand. He was used to being alone. There was no one to miss or to distract him from working hard and rising to the next level.

He'd built armor around himself for a reason. This was not the time to lower his shield.

Perhaps it never would be.

# CHAPTER 11

*B*elle woke with the sun, as though all night long, her heart had been ticking out the minutes until she could see Calvin again. In no time, she was flying out of her chamber and next door to his, the back of her gown gaping open in anticipation of his nimble fingers along her spine.

He opened the door the moment her knuckles touched the wood, as if he had been on the other side awaiting her knock with the same restless eagerness pulsing in his veins.

He captured her in his arms, swinging her into his chamber and closing the door in a single fluid movement that never failed to take her breath away. Or perhaps what stole her breath was him—his intoxicating kisses, the warmth of his embrace, the hardness of his muscles, the exciting familiarity of his scent, the weakness in her knees as they kissed until the room emptied of air.

"I have missed you," he murmured against her mouth.

She clutched him tighter. "I've missed you more."

"Impossible," he growled.

And then their mouths were too busy to speak. His kisses were the best part of every morning, of every twilight, and every moment between.

Their time in each other's arms was also as temporary as the snowflakes that had ceased falling outside the window.

Everything was almost over now. She'd be lucky if the remaining unpainted sketches lasted until teatime. And then what? Why, without busy-work to occupy their idle hands, anything could happen. She wished she could let it happen.

At last, they broke apart. Belle turned so that Calvin could fasten her gown and so she could catch her breath. Light from the window bathed the manikin, Duke, in the aurora of dawn, making him shimmer like a guardian angel.

"Tea?" Calvin asked when she was safely buttoned up.

She nodded. She always said yes to tea. She suspected she would say yes to anything Calvin asked if she were really who she pretended to be.

But when she departed from Houville, he would not be the only thing she left behind. Mrs. Lépine would be no more, and when she vanished, all the freedoms she'd given Belle would disappear with her.

All that would be left was Lady Isabelle, with her familial responsibilities and her societal expectations and her perpetually disappointed mother.

Now that Belle had had her holiday, her chance to playact at a life that was not hers to have, it was time to stop disappointing her mother and live up to her name. She would marry whichever lord her family selected for her and be the best mistress his household had ever seen, as was her duty.

When a kitchen maid brought her chocolate in bed every "morning" at half past noon, Belle would try not to be nostalgic for the days when she'd curled up in a battered wingback chair before a tiny fireplace, as Calvin set a kettle of water to boil above the flames.

She would miss sharing tea from a single cup far more than she'd ever missed the thoughtless luxury of her morning chocolate. She would miss the smile that played on his lips every time he looked at her, as if the mere fact of having her inside his chamber filled his heart with happiness, as it did her. She would miss *him*.

But keeping on was not a choice. No matter how unfair Belle found the strictures and prejudices of high society, no matter how much she chafed at the rules and expectations, she understood them. Society was what she knew and where she belonged.

She would not destroy her own reputation and damage that of her beloved family by willfully engaging in behavior that would bring harsh judgment, ridicule, and mockery upon them all. Nor could she bear to prove herself as unthinking and unworthy as her parents had always feared she would be. The look on her mother's face, if Belle were to develop a *tendre* for the son of her old modiste... Disappointment was even worse than wrath.

Belle *would* make her family proud this time. There was no mystery in how to do so. Mother was happy to lecture her on the precise steps at length. All Belle had to do was obey, as a proper lady ought, and a good daughter would do without question.

That she felt more fake as Lady Isabelle when acting the role that she was born to play, than she did when painting playbills under her pseudonym Mr. Brough or drinking tea in the early morning light as Mrs. Lépine—well, none of that signified. She was not Mr. Brough, and she was not Mrs. Lépine, and she would have to give up all such nonsense in order to become the well-respected lady she was meant to be.

No matter what her foolish heart might wish.

"How is the light?" Calvin asked once the tea had been drunk and there was nothing else to do but get to work.

Nothing except more kisses, perhaps. Was it wrong that Belle would have preferred to do that?

"The light is glorious," she answered. "I'll have the last illustrations finished in no time."

"I've finished all the prototypes," he admitted. "Save for one greatcoat's missing buttons. I'll dress Duke in each design one last time, to ensure every stitch is perfect."

Belle had no doubt every stitch was more than perfect, but she was glad to have Calvin's attention diverted elsewhere for a time. It gave her the opportunity to slip the watercolors she had painted of him measuring and cutting and sewing into the pile of finished illustrations.

He would find them after she was gone. He admired each sketch as she finished it, and had mentioned he would not review them again until his meeting with his partner. She hoped the gift would bring a smile to his lips one more time.

When she was back before her easel, he glanced up from his manikin.

"You do realize how talented you are, don't you?"

Her cheeks flushed with pleasure. "Thank you."

"Incredibly skilled." His gaze was earnest. "You would have no problem selling your work."

An indelicate snort escaped her nose.

He frowned. "I understood you had not yet attempted to publish a collection of your art?"

"Not a book," she agreed. "I tried to find work as an artist throughout London but all I earned for my efforts was laughter. Right in my face."

He shook his head. "A single glance at your art—"

"There were no glances at my art," she explained gently. "There were glances at my face, at my gown, at my age, at my name. The men in charge were much too busy to humor the whims of a silly young woman."

"Their loss," he growled.

"Not exactly," she admitted. "They are using my work, although they've no idea it's me they employ. A certain reclusive 'Mr. Brough' submits his art by post."

"You should tell them." His eyes were dark with

anger. "Throw their prejudices in their ignorant faces. It's your work. You deserve to have your name on it. Not a pseudonym. *You*."

She could do no such thing, of course. Her first act upon reaching Cressmouth would be to write to Mr. Brough's employers, regretfully expressing an old man's desire to retire from service.

The book of Christmas illustrations, on the other hand... No, not even that. Mother would be horrified, and who knew how potential suitors might react? She'd waited this long. Waiting until she secured her husband's permission—if indeed her future lord would grant such a petition—wouldn't change things in the least.

"Obviously, Jonathan and I will credit your work with your name on these illustrations," Calvin assured her.

She stared at him in terror.

"Credit how?" she stammered. "I thought you would only be using a handful of these in your presentation to your investors."

"That's what I thought, as well. And then I saw the finished product. These are wonderful, Belle. Jonathan would have to be a fool not to want to use them in the final catalog, and Jonathan is no fool. Once we've made our selections, I'll let you know, and we can work out proper compensation."

"I don't want compensation." Rather, she did not want him to seek her out. "I give them all to you freely to use as you like."

"Please recognize your worth, Belle." His voice

was quiet steel, his gaze unrelenting. "Your work has value and so do you."

Oh, why did life have to be so muddled? She would *love* to see her name on a project as destined for greatness as Fit for a Duke: *Lady Isabelle, illustrator*.

But she could not allow any such thing to occur. As much as she wished she did not have to hide her true self behind false names, now more than ever she could not risk Calvin learning her true identity. He could place it on the cover of a nationally-available catalogue out of misplaced chivalry and ruin her life.

That was, if his warm feelings toward her did not immediately evaporate upon discovering her a highborn lady. He had made no pretense of his opinions about the upper classes, and his wish to have nothing to do with the beau monde beyond the world of fashion.

That Belle was exactly the type of spoilt young lady who might have once employed his mother... that Belle's own mother had indeed been one of the fine duchesses who frequented her modiste's establishment without ever once inquiring about Mrs. McAlistair's life or progeny, because such details would have been beneath a duchess's notice...

He could never know. When they left the posting house, she must disappear just like the snow.

"There," she said, the word scratching from her throat. "I've completed the final illustration."

He hastened to her side and said everything she'd ever hoped to hear anyone say about her talent with a paintbrush. She would miss that as much as the tea and kisses. Being appreciated for what she could do, rather than for who she'd been born.

After peppering her with lighthearted kisses, Calvin pulled back, his brown eyes twinkling. "I've finished something for you, as well."

She clapped her hands together. "Is it a button-less greatcoat?"

"It is not, minx." He retrieved a package wrapped in brown paper from beside the sofa, and handed the parcel to her. "Open it."

"It feels like Christmas," she said with a nervous laugh, and picked at the twine until it unraveled, and the paper shell revealed its pearl.

Inside was a dazzling frock of deep blue satin and celestial silk, trimmed with a sumptuous, delicate ruff.

"*Is* it Christmas?" she breathed in wonder. "Calvin, this is beautiful. How did you—"

"It's *functional*," he corrected, but his chest had expanded, and his eyes shone with pleasure. "It may *look* like the finest day dress the world has ever seen—and you'd be right—but it closes with an interlocking hash of ribbon beneath a secret panel under the bodice, allowing the wearer to tighten or unfasten it at will."

She narrowed her eyes to hide her laughter. "You could have fashioned me a self-closing dress at any time?"

"I *did* do it at any time," he assured her. "I finished five days ago."

She arched a brow. "And didn't tell me?"

"Your rules, not mine," he reminded her with exaggerated innocence. "I signed a contract that said, 'nothing but buttons.' Even with the verbal 'just kisses' amendment, I was clearly overstepping my—"

She shut him up with a kiss.

"You just didn't want me to stop needing you to unbutton me," she accused.

"Well, yes," he said. "Obviously, that. I'm going to accidentally spill tea on the gown here in a moment so that I can sob, '*Oh no*, woe is me, I shall have to continue undressing you with my bare hands. How could Fate be so cruel as to place this beautiful woman back into my arms...'"

She returned to his arms of her own volition.

"I will throttle you if you allow any evil to befall this gorgeous gown," she warned him.

"Perhaps we should have Duke wear it for safekeeping," Calvin said brightly, gesturing toward his manikin. "I doubt Nottingvale would mind overmuch."

Belle's stomach turned to ice.

"What did you just say?" she asked, her voice faint.

"Oh." Calvin waved a hand, as if brushing her concern away. "The Duke of Nottingvale is our initial investor. He provided the funds for the prototypes, and the measurements for the manikin. Fit for a Duke isn't hyperbole—it's modeled after the real-life Duke of Nottingvale, who I hope will be so impressed with our work and vision that he will invest significantly more and become our partner for life."

Belle's *brother?* Calvin's partner for *life?*

Her head swam with panic, her breaths shallow when they came at all. Had she believed living beneath Vale's shadow was dreadful *before?* Now she definitely could have nothing to do with Calvin's project, not even under a pseudonym. And she especially couldn't be anywhere the two of them might be at the same time.

"When did you say you were meeting..." *My brother.* "...His Grace?"

"On the twenty-third of December," Calvin replied. "Two days before Twelve-tide."

Before the party, Belle realized in relief. Vale would never mix business with pleasure. All the same, she would not attend until after Calvin left, to be safe. She could stay with Angelica until there was no doubt all danger had passed.

She would have spent this past fortnight with Angelica anyway, had it not been for the snowstorm. Belle was simply moving the dates of her visit. Angelica would not mind, and Vale and his guests would not notice. Belle wasn't the reason they attended the party.

"Have you met His Grace before?" she asked as casually as possible.

Calvin made a face. "I'd sworn to have nothing further to do with the beau monde at all, and now look at me, arranging private meetings. No, we haven't met. I've corresponded with his tailor, which is how I got the measurements for the manikin. My partner Jonathan is the one who has been communicating with Nottingvale. I suppose that will all change now."

"I suppose so," she echoed faintly.

It was a good thing she had harbored no ridiculous secret fantasies about running off with Calvin. The track would lead right back home to her family. There would be no pseudonym to hide behind. Even as Mrs. McAlistair, every day would still be nothing but Nottingvale, Nottingvale, Nottingvale. She'd already inadvertently painted illustrations for a company that turned out to be both his likeness and namesake.

Her family's orbit was inescapable, even under an assumed identity.

"I should go," she stammered. "I need to check on Ursula."

Calvin cupped the side of her face. "You'll be back for sunset?"

She nodded. Of course she would be back. Her family had won—they always won—but they hadn't won *yet*.

"I'll pick up supper from the kitchen," she said. "And a bottle of wine."

After one last kiss, she placed her new gown in her room with care, then hurried downstairs to place their supper order and ask about Ursula.

For the first time since arriving, she was told Ursula had improved enough to be allowed company.

"And just in time," Mildred chirped as she led Belle back to the erstwhile sickroom. "Now that the snow has stopped, teams of men have spent all day clearing the roads. By this time tomorrow, the Hoot & Holly will have completely different customers under its roof."

Belle swallowed hard. Once upon a time, escaping the shabby posting house was all she'd wished to do. Now it was the last thing she wanted. Without the excuse of snow, Calvin no longer had a reason to stay.

Christmas was just beginning, but Belle's holiday had come to an end. It was time to wake up from the dream.

Ursula's eyes lit up when Belle entered the room. "Lady—"

"I'm Mrs. Lépine," Belle whispered as she enveloped Ursula in a quick embrace. "I'm so pleased to find you looking like yourself again."

"I see you've missed me something dreadful," Ursula said with a laugh, plucking at Belle's sleeve. "Where are your stays? Oh, of course you can't manage them alone. I've no idea how you even secured this gown. I'm so sorry to have abandoned you like that."

"You didn't abandon me," Belle chided her maid, trying not to be hurt by the *of course you can't manage* comments. No one ever thought she could manage anything, and until this past week, Belle had believed them.

But she *had* managed, hadn't she? She'd managed to make friends with a handsome stranger. She'd managed to become an artist-for-hire, a temporary assistant performing a necessary and valued service.

She'd managed to get her life and her heart tangled into bits.

Ursula flung back her blanket and swung her feet to the floor. "I'm coming with you."

"What?" Belle jumped back in alarm.

Ursula couldn't possibly resume her duties *now*. Not when a bottle of wine and romantic supper was being prepared for a certain shared sunset on the third floor.

"Why don't you rest for one more night," Belle suggested. "You'll be very busy at my brother's cottage." Or would be, if Belle had any intention of attending the party. "Resuming your duties in the morning will be soon enough."

Ursula frowned. "But don't you need—"

Belle *did* need. She was trying to fathom out a way to have what she wanted, if only for a few more stolen moments.

"Stay here until I send for you," she instructed. "I'll make certain you get your sleep before we set out."

"Oh, are the roads free again?" Ursula lay back on her pillow and closed her eyes. "You must be so happy."

Belle was very happy, if by "happy" one meant *distraught*.

Her time left with Calvin could be counted in hours. Unbeknownst to them at the time, they'd already had their last day. All that was left was tonight. One chance to experience what it would have been like to have everything she wanted.

She wouldn't let it slip away.

# CHAPTER 12

*C*alvin tried not to think about the sunset's bittersweet beauty. He adored these moments snuggled on the sofa with Belle in his arms, but the setting of the sun also signaled her imminent departure. Soon she would set down her barely touched glass of wine, they would kiss one last time, and then he'd unbutton her gown and say good-bye.

She wouldn't need him in the morning. She might not *be* here in the morning. A footman had brought him the good news hours ago along with a hot bath: The snow had stopped. The roads were clear. Calvin and the other guests were trapped no more.

Huzzah.

It wasn't that Calvin wished to avoid his trip to Cressmouth. He'd been waiting for an opportunity like this his entire life. Working toward it night and day, whilst he ate, in his sleep. He had tried so hard and so long. He had let nothing stand in his way. Success was close enough to taste.

So was Belle. He had tasted her lips countless times as the sun dipped behind the endless sea of snow-capped evergreens. He could not stop kissing her, no matter how he tried. Perhaps for a few seconds, a long moment, and then he would turn to her or she would turn to him or they would turn to each other at the same time, hungry for something far more filling than a candlelit dinner could provide.

She looked at him now and the familiar flutter tickled somewhere deep in his chest. He would never be used to the curve of her eyelashes, the rosy blush of cheeks kissed by the setting sun. He wished *he* could paint, so that he could capture her just like this; mussed and thoroughly kissed, and a mere heartbeat away from the next kiss.

They barely managed to set down their wine glasses on this surface or that before their mouths and bodies crashed together and they were back in each other's arms. What allure could a sunset offer when he had Belle to hold? He adored her softness, her sweetness, although tonight her kisses were different. They had not been hesitant with one another since their first embrace, but these kisses were hungrier than before, naked, incendiary. This was no kiss good-bye. These were kisses that started a fire and stoked the flames higher.

She pulled her mouth from his but just barely, her lush lower lip brushing against his as she said, "I'm leaving in the morning. This is our last evening together. I want... I want to make it count."

Ah. So, it *was* a kiss good-bye. But they would not be stopping there.

He slid his fingers deeper into her hair, kissed her until they both gasped for air. "Tell me what you want."

"I want everything." Her hot gaze did not waver from his. "I want *you*. Just for tonight."

"Then you will have me."

He scooped her into his arms to carry her into the bedchamber. For a second, he could not bear to allow her out of his embrace, if only to tumble to the center of his bed. How many times had he dreamt of having her exactly there? How was he supposed to walk away forever? How could one night ever be enough?

"Let me undress you," he said gruffly, setting her beside the bed rather than on top of it.

She peered up at him with a half-smile. "One last time?"

"No." He tried not to question why the words *one last time* chafed so much. "For the first time."

He had unbuttoned her a dozen times, and buttoned her just as many. But for as familiar as the tips of his fingers were with the nape of her neck, the soft curve of her spine, unbuttoning was all that they had allowed themselves.

Until tonight.

His body tightened in anticipation as he freed each ivory pearl from its silken slit. This time, when he reached the final button, she would stay right here in his bed. He would uncover every inch of her soft flesh, thread by thread, and take her until they both came undone.

He lowered his mouth to her freshly exposed shoulder, pressing his lips to the hollow above her collarbone as he let the delicate gown slide down her curves to the floor in a whisper of fallen silk.

She did not try to catch the material as it fell, and instead turned to face him, the pulse at her neck fluttering.

She wore no stays, and he was glad of it. Her plump breasts were right there, nipples puckering invitingly beneath the gossamer linen of her chemise. He plundered her mouth as he cupped her breasts, enjoying their soft weight as he teased her pert nipples until she fumbled at his neckcloth, as if eager to do to him everything he was doing to her.

He let her rip off his cravat, his jacket, his waistcoat. Any other moment, he would have treated each item gingerly, keeping his bespoke clothing and her expensive gown carefully folded and safe on some wardrobe shelf far from the bed.

Tonight, he didn't care if each seam ripped asunder. He would resew every stitch in the morning if he had to, or better yet, they'd spend the dawn naked, limbs tangled together beneath the sheets. Who needed clothes when they had a bed and a woman like Belle to share it?

No, not a woman *like* Belle. There was no one else he wanted in his arms. No one else he wanted in his life. A few stolen hours could never be enough. He would prove it to her kiss by kiss, lick by lick, stroke by stroke.

He yanked off his favorite cambric shirt, flinging it to a far corner. There was too much material still between them. He slid the soft linen of her shift up her thighs, over the curve of her hips, her waist, her breasts, and over her head. He tossed the flimsy chemise to the floor and lifted Belle up and into the center of the bed.

She was so beautiful, part of him could not bear to cover up her delectable body with his. So, he did not. He lay on his side beside her and dipped his mouth to her nipple.

With his hand, he explored the rest of her, not resting until his fingers slid to cup her slick heat. Her legs tensed about him for a brief second until his fingertip began a lazy pattern that soon had her hips bucking against his hand in quest for more.

Of course he would give it to her. He alternated teasing circles with shallow dips inside. She gripped his hair, clutching him tight to her bosom as if he could ever wish to be anywhere else. This was just the beginning.

*Tonight* was only the beginning.

He could not possibly be expected to walk away from...

Love.

The realization hit him as her breath quickened, and her body strained into his hand. He was in love, damn it all. And not in a position to give her more than the one night she asked for... yet.

He slid his hand from between her legs and she whimpered.

"Calvin..."

"Here I am." He lowered himself until his

tongue could take over for his hand. He needed to taste her, to feel her thighs tremble about him.

What if they could have this *every* night and every day? They needn't wait until Fit for a Duke was delivered to every breakfast table in England.

As soon as his presentation was over and the duke's investment safely transferred, Calvin could offer Belle a secure future in addition to passionate nights. He could not tell her his plans yet—only once his company was on solid footing would he have the means to sway her from one night of pleasure to all the rest of the nights; a *lifetime* of pleasure.

He would make himself a catch worthy of her. Then there would be no more need for good-byes.

# CHAPTER 13

*B*elle pressed her knuckles to her lips to contain the gasps of pleasure coming from her mouth, but it was no use. Her arms fell bonelessly to her sides, her head lolling helplessly into his pillow. Calvin knelt between her thighs, his mouth and tongue feasting on her in ways she'd never known possible.

She was no stranger to the delicious pressure building inside her. Her fingers had found this spot before, had brought her to the edge and over, but never like this. She felt splayed open and worshipped, vulnerable and powerful.

He could do anything at all, and she would let him, would beg him not to stop. But all he wanted was to bring her pleasure. To devour her until she could no longer think, no longer feel the soft pillow or the woolen blanket or the cool air against her bared limbs because nothing else existed but his tongue and his fingers and the building, building pressure. Yes, right there, exactly like that, she was going to—

She fractured into a thousand pieces, her muscles convulsing, her legs trapping him to her, then falling limp to his shoulders. She should be sated. She *was* sated. But her body was greedy and wanted more, wanted *him*. She wanted everything. Even if all they could have was one last stolen moment.

*Especially* because all they had was tonight.

She could count their remaining hours on her fingertips. It was not enough, but it would have to be. She would make it so. Tomorrow he would pursue his dreams and she would return to obedience and duty, but in this precise moment they still had each other, and she was far from ready to let him go.

She reached for him to pull him to her, but he would not be rushed. He pressed lazy, open-mouthed kisses to the crease of her thigh, to the curve of her hip, to the dip at her waist, to the valley between her breasts, to the peak of her nipple.

Only when she could feel the pressure rising within her once more did she realize his hand was between her legs, teasing her with sensual promises the same way his mouth and teeth and tongue did to her breasts and nipples. She wanted more. She wanted it all.

When she could feel herself rising close to the crest again, she tugged him to her. "Calvin— I want—"

He needed no explanation. His eyes glowed in the moonlight; his body hotter than any fire. He eased himself from her just long enough to cast his trousers off the edge of the bed and then he was back, hotter than before, harder, bigger. He positioned himself at her entrance, the hard, pulsing length of him rubbing where his fingers and tongue had been, making the same wicked promise.

She was through with promises. She wanted action; she wanted life. She wanted it to be *him*.

His mouth was hot on hers, but he broke the kiss long enough to say, "Are you certain?"

Her heart clanged as she nodded.

That was sweet of him, to ask. He thought her a worldly widow, and nonetheless wanted to be sure she—

He drove inside with one long thrust and Belle could not keep her cry of pain and surprise trapped inside her throat.

He froze at once, his face filled with alarm. "Am I... Are you..."

"I'm fine," she managed, and it was almost true. Already the initial pain was a dull ache, leaving her instead with a not unpleasant sensation of fullness and promise. "It's just... It's been a while since..."

A long while like *never*, but she didn't want him to stop now. She didn't want to explain herself, didn't want the guilt, the recriminations, the weight of who she was supposed to be and what sort of man she was and was not supposed to want.

She didn't want any regrets at all, because for her there would not be any. There was no one else she would rather lie with, no one else worth saving herself for. All other men would have to live up to *him*, not the other way round. And she would forever find them lacking. No one could ever replace Calvin.

He began to move, slowly, carefully, eyes open and fixed on hers.

He need not worry. The only ache left now was the one he'd built with his mouth and fingers. A swirling, rising, pressure that stoked higher with every stroke. Her hips found the rhythm, and she wrapped her legs about him to meet him again and again, intermingling deep and slow with fast and hungry. Their kisses were just as ravenous.

Oh, how were they ever meant to limit themselves to just one night? She wanted all his nights, all his days, in his bedchamber and out. She wanted to breathe in the same air, feel the same sun on her skin, share the same meals. She wanted to wake up every morning in his arms and return to bed every night just like this, their bodies joined together, their hands and mouths insatiable for each other.

There didn't exist a number of nights that could ever be enough. No quantity of days or months or years could extinguish the impression he had made in her heart, a mold that only he could fit.

Here came the crest again—this time, he would ride it with her. She gripped him close, their kisses punctuated by gasps as her muscles contracted around him. At the last pulse, he jerked his hips from hers as his seed spilled hot against her thigh.

He rolled onto his back, taking her with him, away from the wet proof of their lovemaking and into his warm, solid embrace. He held her close, his breathing as labored as hers, his heartbeat just as thunderous.

He pressed a kiss to her hair, then lay his cheek against the spot he'd kissed and cradled her close. She had never felt so precious, so cherished. She did not trust herself to speak, lest she say words that must forever remain unspoken.

Despite her very best efforts, she *loved* him, would always love him. That it was forbidden did not dampen her ardor. He was in her arms, inside her body, and still she longed for more. For forever.

She couldn't keep him, of course she knew that. Her family would be apoplectic at the very idea. Her reputation! The family's good name! Nor would she put Calvin through the hell the Nottingvale family would rain down upon him for daring to steal a kiss, much less her heart. It would be the end of Calvin's dreams, not the beginning of a new life. The best thing she could do for him, for them both, was walk away and never look back.

But not until morning. She would not allow the fate of their births to steal a single extra moment.

She awoke in his arms, the pink light of dawn caressing them both.

His heartbeat was slow and steady, his muscular form warm and familiar. She wanted to wake him up and make love all over again, to carry the secret ache between her legs with her when she left, like a brand marking her as his.

But she was not his, and they were out of time.

Dawn meant Ursula would awaken at any moment, and hurry upstairs to help her mistress into her carriage dress for the journey ahead. Belle could not allow her maid to arrive and find the chamber empty. They had to leave without raising any eyebrows at all.

She slipped from Calvin's arms and padded about the room as quietly as possible, retying her stockings, slipping on her chemise, struggling with the gown she'd worn in the hopes of dazzling him into bed.

"Come here." His voice was gruff, indulgent.

She whirled to face him, her cheeks heating. How long had he been watching her? Was it possible he had not been sleeping at all, but just lying there, holding her to his chest in silence as the sun poked above the evergreens?

She presented him with her spine as she'd done every morning and every evening since her arrival, but this time on shaking legs. She could not be near him without wanting to kiss him, to press her body into his, to fall back onto the mattress and forget whatever it was the sunrise wished to demand of her.

When the last button slipped into place, she stepped away from him rather than into his embrace. It was time to say good-bye. The distance between them would soon be insurmountable.

"Thank you," she said softly. "For everything."

He frowned and rose from the edge of the bed. His lack of clothing did not make him look naked, but rather more powerful, more dangerous. Irresistible.

She would have to be strong.

"It's morning," she babbled. "I have to go."

"Do you?" He was suddenly right before her, touching his thumb to her cheekbone.

She swallowed. "My maid will arrive soon. I must... I must go."

"Will you be back for breakfast? You can bring Ursula." His finger traced the outer shell of her ear. "I promise not to ravish you until the next time we're alone."

She took a deep breath. "There won't be a next time. This is good-bye."

"For now," he agreed, and took her hands in his. "Belle—"

She closed her eyes. "Don't say it."

"I'm not in a position to offer marriage—"

She opened her eyes, sagging in relief.

"—but I will be soon," he continued, his gaze earnest and unwavering. "Thanks to all your help, I know our presentation will be a success. Once we've secured the Duke of Nottingvale's investment and endorsement, Fit for a Duke can provide—"

"No," she said. "I mean, yes. Fit for a Duke will be a smashing success and so will you. But I cannot be part—"

"You won't be *part*, Belle." His eyes were fierce, but his thumbs tender against the backs of her trembling hands. "You're everything. Once the company is stable, it won't require much of my time. If you don't like my cottage, I'll be able to afford a bigger one, with a parlor dedicated exclusively to your art, or whatever it is that would please you most. I don't just want to provide for you. I want us to—"

It sounded lovely.

It was impossible.

"No. I..." She shook her head. "You don't understand. It's not just me, it's..."

"Oh." He cupped her cheek. "I've been insensitive. Forgive me. I'm not trying to replace your first husband, Belle. Your memories with him—"

"Stop," she choked out. This could not go on any longer.

He was proposing to a better version of herself than even existed. There was absolutely no reason at all for Mrs. Lépine not to leap into his arms with eager acceptance. He was everything she could want in a husband, first or second or otherwise.

But she was not Mrs. Lépine. She was the daughter of a duke, the sister of a duke, the despair of the current duchess of Nottingvale.

She would hurt Calvin more by keeping up the charade of being an independent widow who could make choices on her own without having to consider their impact on a centuries-long dynasty. Mrs. Lépine was free to say yes, which would make her *no* sting all the worse.

Belle was not free. She had never been free. And now she'd gone too far. It was past time to be honest with him. Once he knew the truth, he would no longer want her. She had a talent for disappointing the people she loved most.

"I know I am not the finest catch at the moment. But as soon as I *can* give you the life you deserve, I want to be the man who does it." His thumb caressed her cheek. "Will you think about it?"

Belle would think about this moment for the rest of her life. She took a deep, shuddering breath.

"Calvin... there's something you should know."

# CHAPTER 14

*C*alvin brushed a stray wisp of hair from Belle's cheek. There was something she felt he should know?

"I think I know what it is," he said gently, embarrassed that he hadn't noticed sooner. "I didn't realize you were a virgin until it was too late, and I was already inside you. Forgive me, Belle. It never occurred to me that you and the late Mr. Lépine did not consummate—"

Her cheeks flushed scarlet. "That's not it at all." The blush spread further. "That is to say, yes, I was a virgin, but not due to any failure to consummate on Mr. Lépine's part."

He frowned. "Then how—"

"There *is* no Mr. Lépine," she burst out, her face miserable. "I'm not a widow. I've never been married. I'm—"

He dropped his hand from her cheek. "You lied to me?"

"I lied to the proprietress." She swallowed visibly. "And yes, to you, and to everyone in this posting house, because the only way to keep one's reputation intact is with the constant presence of a maid—or by not requiring one. Ursula was in the sickroom and there was no one else to play chaperone, so I lied about my name out of desperation."

Calvin scrubbed his face. Well, there. That wasn't so dreadful a fib, was it?

Her alleged widowhood hadn't protected her virtue last night in his bed, but as far as the rest of the posting house knew, nothing untoward had occurred. Her quick thinking had worked. Nor did it change his feelings—or his intentions—toward Belle. He was no less in love with *Miss* Lépine as he had been with *Mrs.* Lépine.

Yet something she'd said niggled at him.

"You lied about your name?" he echoed slowly. "Or just your marital status?"

"I'm still Belle," she hedged, not meeting his eyes until, suddenly, she did, as if rallying courage. "There are no Lépines. I am Lady Isabelle."

"Lady... who?" Calvin took a step back, suddenly aware of his nakedness.

The name did not sound familiar, but then why would it? He was no aristocrat. The only dealings he'd had with the ladies of the ton had been when he'd helped his mother design their trousseaux over a decade ago. He'd never bothered keeping up with the names and titles in *Debrett's Peerage* because he didn't rub shoulders with the nobs, nor did he wish to. Their worlds did not intersect.

Until now.

"Lady Isabelle," he repeated, the syllables sticking to the roof of his mouth like ash.

He had let her see every tiny hidden part of himself, and she hadn't even been honest about her name.

She wasn't who he'd thought she was. No, it was worse than that. She inhabited a world he could only ape. She was silk and gold and diamonds, and he was a cheap facsimile. And she'd known it all along.

Calvin had fallen in love, but *Lady Isabelle* had merely been on holiday. He was a lark, nothing more. She'd been amusing herself with the hapless tailor since that first shared pie, playacting at "commoner" until the snow cleared enough for her to return to her ivory tower.

Of *course* she had said no to his mangled proposal. She had known from the start that what they had meant nothing at all.

He snatched his trousers up from the floor and shoved his leg into the wrinkled nankeen.

"You're angry," she said hesitantly.

He sent her a dark look as he bent to scoop up his shirt.

She wrung her hands. "It's worse than that."

He pulled on his shirt in silence.

"Calvin—"

"Your plan was to walk away and never see each other again, wasn't it? Then there's no need for any more drawn out confessions."

"Just one more," she said in a small voice. "I thought it might be prudent for you to know that I'm... the Duke of Nottingvale's sister."

He staggered backward as though each word had pummeled his solar plexus.

"You thought it *prudent* for me to know that I despoiled the Duke of Nottingvale's virgin sister?" His stomach dipped as gooseflesh rippled across his suddenly clammy skin. "Why wasn't this information prudent *yesterday*, before I had you naked in my bed?"

She stared at him in misery. "I... I wanted..."

"*You* wanted," he spat. "Of course you did. You were raised to only care about your wants, and damn anyone else. I was a toy, not a person. And now you've ruined both of us."

"I didn't know you'd want to make an honest woman of me!" she burst out.

"I'm not sure anyone could do that," he said coldly. He had never felt so foolish.

She thought he would take her and forget her, as she had intended to do with him. It was what she'd *wanted*.

He raked a trembling hand through his hair. It was over. Not just his affair with "Mrs. Lépine" but Fit for a Duke and all it entailed. Belle hadn't stopped with merely breaking his heart. She'd managed to destroy his life's dream for good measure.

"I suppose you'll be at the party," he said dully.

Another fortnight under the same roof, but this time under the watchful eye of one of the most powerful men in England. Jonathan was depending upon him to bring the materials for the presentation, and Nottingvale was relying on him not to despoil his little sister along the way.

There was no way Calvin could go.

"Party?" Belle stammered. "My brother invited you... to stay for Yuletide..."

"Merry Christmas to us all," Calvin said flatly. "The investment will be off once the duke finds out—"

"He *can't* find out." Her eyes were wild. "I'll never tell him. His reaction would be nothing compared to my mother's. She'd never forgive me for sullying the family with... scandal."

Wonderful. Exactly the reaction a man hoped for upon proposing marriage.

Proof that he was of no more value than a clump of mud stuck to her shoe. He was in pain, angry and numb at the realization that everything he'd worked for had disappeared the moment he'd taken her into his arms. He'd hoped they could forge a new future.

Now there would be nothing at all.

"We won't have to tell him," Calvin said with a sigh. "He'll know. We cannot possibly keep up the charade of total strangers whilst trapped under the same roof for an entire fortnight. *You* might be that talented of an actress, but I am not."

"I won't go," she said quickly. "I'd already decided not to go before we even... I'll stay with my friend Angelica. I won't let on that we've met, much less made love. Don't worry."

"Don't *worry?*" he repeated in disbelief. "More futures than just mine are hanging on a thread. Nottingvale is a powerful duke whom I'd hoped would become a trusted business partner. You're asking me to *lie* to him, not just for the length of one party, but for the rest of our lives. My conscience would be better off if I admitted the truth up front, and let the chips fall where they may."

"You *can't*," she burst out in horror, face pale. "I'll be ruined if you do, and besides you... you signed a contract..."

He let out a humorless chuckle.

"The contract was in regard to a Mrs. Lépine, who, it turns out, does not exist. The document is worthless, and you know it." He led her to the door on stiff legs. "It seems you'll just have to trust the discretion of a lowly tailor."

## CHAPTER 15

*T*he Hoot & Holly posting house was a snowy smudge far in the distance when Belle finally stopped trying to steal furtive glances out of the window as the horses drew the coach higher and higher up the twisting evergreen-lined road to Cressmouth.

She'd *known* it couldn't last. And then it didn't last. Exactly as anticipated. Yet she could not help but feel like a thief fleeing through the night in an attempt to outrun the future.

It wasn't the future that scared her, Belle told herself. How could it? Her destiny had been foretold since the moment of her birth. It was as unavoidable as the air she breathed.

She was running from Calvin. From the hurt in his eyes, the bitter disappointment, the well-deserved anger. She was running from *Belle, what were you thinking?* because contrary to everyone's beliefs, she *had* been thinking.

She'd been thinking any woman would be lucky to have a man like Calvin in her life. She'd

163

been thinking how unfair it was that she could never be "any woman" and instead was forced to be a predictable, respectable lady. She was thinking no Mayfair terrace could ever offer a view half as marvelous as watching the sunset sparkle off the falling snow from the comfortable warmth of Calvin's arms.

She was thinking that if she could do it all over again, she *would*. Every single minute in his company was permanently engraved upon her heart. Their kisses, yes, the lovemaking, of course, but also the companionship of roasting chestnuts over a tiny fire, the silliness of sharing tea from a single cup, the camaraderie of working together not on embroidered handkerchiefs that would molder in a basket of more of the same, but on a project that *meant* something, that could change lives.

She'd felt more important in those moments than she ever had waltzing through Almack's, or riding an open barouche through Hyde Park at the precise hour when everyone would see her and gawk.

She had felt important to *Calvin*. No, she had *been* important, and then ruined everything by admitting who and what she was. His gorgeous speech in which he'd expressed his desire to become a man worthy of her was laughable not because he was beneath her, but because she was not a woman who deserved *him*.

The last thing she'd wanted was to see the affection vanish from his eyes, but he deserved the truth. He was bound to find out eventually, one way or the other, and she would much rather he hear it from her. She owed him that much, at least. He'd given her more life in a fortnight as Mrs. Lépine than she'd enjoyed in the four-and-twenty years prior.

"Well?" Ursula said softly. Belle had told her the whole story.

*Most* of the story.

"I did the right thing," Belle mumbled. She smoothed the gown Calvin had made for her, rather than meet her maid's too-perceptive gaze.

"Which part felt like the right part?" Ursula persisted. "When you were there with him, or when you left?"

Belle didn't answer. She didn't have to. Ursula had made an irrelevant point. That Belle had preferred her false persona with Calvin to her real life as a Nottingvale did not signify. Being a Nottingvale was the only thing that had ever signified. She'd been taught that before she knew her own name.

But now, something else also signified. Calvin mattered very much. The business partner Belle had never met mattered. Fit for a Duke mattered. And all the future customers who would look and feel their best thanks to Calvin and his affordable, fashionable couture.

By staying out of his way from now until forever, she was doing all of those people a grand favor.

The road had forked. He would go his way and she would go hers.

Ursula twisted her lips. "You look miserable."

Belle balled her hands at her hips. "Thank you."

Ursula tried again. "If you didn't want to leave—"

"He didn't want me to *stay*," Belle reminded her. "He wanted the widow Lépine, who doesn't exist."

Ursula shook her head. "He wanted *you*."

"And what would the duchess say to that?" Belle snapped. "You've heard Mother pontificate as many times as I have. She would be mortified if I accepted the hand of a noble-born second son, much less a common tailor. Heirs presumptive are not good enough for Lady Isabelle. A Nottingvale only accepts the very best. We give the gossips no fodder."

"Is that what he is?" Ursula asked. "A common tailor?"

"No." The word exhaled from her lungs in a defeated little sigh. Belle's shoulders slumped. "He's as uncommon as a shooting star among glow-worms. I'll never find someone else who shines half as bright. But nor can I bring shame to my family. I don't want to cause them any pain, and I'm tired of being a disappointment. I want Mother to be proud of me, for once."

"To hear her brag about you instead of your brother?" Ursula asked with far too much perspicacity.

"Correct," Belle replied defiantly. "Just once, I'd like to be the one that sparkles. I've lived in the Nottingvale shadow my entire life; I've been a disappointment since birth. Even if Mother somehow gave Calvin and me her blessing, I

166

would not escape Vale's shadow, but be thrust deeper inside it."

Of course "Fit for a Duke" couldn't simply be a clever metaphor. It had to be modeled quite literally after an actual duke. Her elder brother, the handsomest, wealthiest, most eligible bachelor in all of England.

Fit for a Duke *was* Vale, just like it was Calvin, and his business partner MacLean. All three pieces were inextricable. Belle was the part that didn't belong. She had spent her entire life looking for the place where she *did* belong. She loved Calvin and her brother too much to lock herself into a situation where she would resent them for life. She could not marry her brother's business partner and live permanently in that shadow.

"You're stronger than that," Ursula said. "You don't need your mother's approbation. You need to give yourself your own."

Belle glared at her. "A Nottingvale—"

"—should do as a Nottingvale pleases," Ursula cut in. "You've always done as your mother pleases, as your father pleases, as your brother pleases. When will you get to do as *you* please?"

"Never," Belle said listlessly. "An obedient daughter does as her parents decree until the day she weds, upon which she becomes an obedient wife who does as her husband bids."

Ursula lifted her brows. "Does Mr. McAlistair wish to 'bid' you?"

No. He wished to bed her, which Belle also wanted. He wished to spend mornings with her, and noon meals, and tea time, and sunsets, and then find themselves back in each other's arms. He wished to work *with* her, not to command her. He wanted to put her name in a place of honor on his catalogue, to give credit where he felt it was due.

Ursula tilted her head. "You've been trained to give up when people tell you no. But what if you didn't?"

Belle stared at her.

She wasn't afraid to say what she wanted, but she never got to have it. *No* was the most common word Father had ever spoken to her. *No* was always at the tip of Mother's tongue. *No, no, no* was all she'd heard from the publishing houses and entertainment venues who had refused to even open Belle's portfolio. After the success of "Mr. Brough," why hadn't she confronted them with the proof of her talent?

"Don't wait for a hero," Ursula said softly. "Be one."

Even with Calvin, Belle had negotiated the wrong direction with the button contract. He'd offered to pay her to paint, and she'd demurred and done it for free. He'd offered to credit her as a valued contributor, and she'd brushed that off, as well. Belle told herself no just as often as she heard it from other people.

Ursula's gaze was sharp. "You must fight for what you want."

"I want Calvin." The words scratched from Belle's throat, but they weren't the whole story.

Status did not matter. All people were worthy, regardless of their bloodlines. Belle had met enough so-called gentlemen to know that Calvin was in a class of his own. He deserved to have every dream come true. Belle wanted to believe she deserved the same.

"I want it all," she admitted. "I don't want to sparkle just once, but for the rest of my life. I want to be an artist who gets paid for her work. I want my signature to be my name, not a pseudonym. I want my work and my name to be as meaningful as my husband's. I want to be a *team*, not a doll or a pet."

Ursula tilted her head. "Is that something he could give you?"

"It's what he tried to give me." Belle's chest felt empty. "I ruined it."

"Did you ruin it?" Ursula asked. "How can you know you've caused irreparable harm if you haven't tried to make any repairs?"

"If... if I chase after Calvin, the next place I'll see my name will be in a scandal column. No lord would want me. My reputation will be ruined."

Ursula shrugged. "Your mother cares about that. Do you?"

"I...do not." Belle gave a startled little laugh. "What good is 'Lady Isabelle's' precious reputation if all my best work is under a pseudonym? Maybe *she's* the one who doesn't exist and never has. I would trade my status as a lady for one of an artist married to the man she loves."

Ursula grinned at her. "Then do it. Don't take 'no' for an answer."

Belle's pulse quickened, a sudden syncopated staccato.

She might not have the power to win the battle, but she had the power to try. She could no longer be afraid of failure. Calvin was worth the risk. Belle was worth the risk. So was his business, her art, their future.

It was too late to return to the Hoot & Holly to apologize. He had left first. She had cowered in her tiny guest chamber until she heard his door, his footsteps, and then nothing.

She did not have his address. There was no direction where she might send a letter or pay a call. But she did know where he intended to spend the Yuletide.

The question was whether she could convince Calvin that Lady Isabelle was just as worthy as Mrs. Lépine... and convince her powerful brother not to retaliate against the tailor who had stolen his sister's heart.

CHAPTER 16

*B*y the time Calvin reached the Duke of Nottingvale's charming holiday cottage, snow was once again beginning to fall. He prayed he would be able to leave straight after the presentation. He could no longer imagine himself making merry in a Christmas village full of strangers.

Well, no, that wasn't entirely true. Calvin was very good at disappearing in a room full of strangers. The person he didn't want to see was Belle. Even if the presentation went well, and the duke signed a contract detailing his patronage, the moment he suspected Calvin had been anywhere near his sister...

His muscles tightened. The duke would not find out. Calvin had worked too bloody hard on this dream for too long. Fit for a Duke was too important to him and to Jonathan and to all their soon to be well-dressed customers for Calvin to preemptively walk away. He was reclusive, but not a coward. He'd come here to fight for his dream.

Calvin and Jonathan would take this moment of privacy to prepare an impeccable presentation before the duke arrived, and then after they secured his investment and his endorsement, Calvin need not be present for any additional tête-à-tête. All further arrangements could be handled via post.

He would disappear from Belle's life, just as she'd always intended.

His lungs constricted painfully. He had *tried* to be honorable. He'd given her his heart. She hadn't even given him her true name. His jaw clenched. He would not think about Belle. Not here. Not until he was back in the empty sanctuary of his home.

At the sight of Calvin and his driver alighting from the carriage, a quartet of well-appointed footmen streamed from Nottingvale's cottage to assist with the valises. Calvin handled his manikin Duke himself for safekeeping.

The butler showed them into a large, sunny parlor. Calvin had scarcely positioned Duke in the primary window's best light when Jonathan strode in through the open door.

"My apologies for not arriving on schedule," Calvin said. "The snowstorm had... unexpected consequences. I trust you were not terribly bored in my absence?"

The most peculiar expression crossed Jonathan's handsome, rakish face. It almost looked like... a blush?

"Not too bored." Jonathan's voice was strangled, but he'd turned to busy himself with the unloading of trunks and Calvin could no longer see his face. "We have to hurry."

"We are further along than you might think."

Calvin unsheathed the stack of painted illustrations. They were as stunning as the artist who had painted them. Despite all that had happened, he was proud of the result. Proud of Belle. But he could never look at these prints without remembering all the happy afternoons they'd worked together in harmony... or the cold dawn when her indifference was finally laid bare.

He shoved the stack at Jonathan. "Here. Select your favorites. The duke arrives tomorrow afternoon, is that right? We need to be ready."

"We need to *already* be ready. His Grace arrived an hour ago, and he will join us in the parlor shortly."

Calvin's muscles flinched. "He's *here?*"

Damn the snowstorm! Calvin had lost his heart *and* his sole opportunity to discuss strategy with his business partner prior to the most important meeting Fit for a Duke would face.

"What's this?" Jonathan flipped through the illustrations with obvious surprise. "Had I known you were capable—"

"It wasn't me." Calvin concentrated on dressing Duke so he could not meet Jonathan's gaze. "An... er... assistant lent a hand."

"These are very good." Paper rustled. "We ought to hire the fellow outright."

"Woman," Calvin corrected automatically, and wished he hadn't, for now he would need to explain himself. "She's called... Mrs. Lépine." No.

He would not perpetuate a lie. "It's a pseudonym."

"She can call herself the Queen of England for all I care," Jonathan said. "These are impressive. I particularly admire the candid watercolor series of you designing a custom wardrobe and outfitting your manikin with care."

"Watercolors of *what?*" Calvin spun around and held out a shaking palm.

Jonathan handed him a dozen sheets and resumed his perusal of the painted sketches.

It was indeed an utterly charming series. Calvin, cutting fabric in total concentration, a few pins protruding from the corner of his mouth. Calvin, serene and bathed in sunlight, sewing the fabric into a waistcoat before an instantly recognizable vista of snow-covered evergreens. Calvin, buttoning the waistcoat on Duke, eyes alive with pride and delight because this prototype was already his favorite, and he hadn't even got to the tailcoat yet.

Belle wasn't in any of the behind-the-curtain portraits, yet her presence was in every stroke of the brush, every splash of color.

Calvin swallowed hard. Belle was not indifferent after all. She simply didn't want him enough. Not openly, anyway. Like her book and her playbills, he was something she only dabbled with in secret. Something she would turn her back on in a heartbeat before it could sully her lofty reputation.

He shoved the watercolors back into the

leather portfolio, where they could no longer remind him of her.

Footsteps sounded in the hall, followed by Jonathan's whispered, *"He's here."*

Calvin straightened just as the duke strode into the parlor.

Nottingvale was tall and broad of shoulder. Imposing in the way powerful people often were, when they'd wielded their power since birth and used it as casually as someone else used a pencil. He had the same dark hair as his sister, but his eyes were a bright brown, rather than hazel. And their sharp focus was right on Calvin.

"Calvin," Jonathan said smoothly, "may I present His Grace, the Duke of Nottingvale? Your Grace, this is my business partner, Calvin McAlistair, the genius behind all these fashionable designs."

Calvin performed his best bow.

Nottingvale swept past him. "Yes, well, I'm afraid this will have to be quick. Such unpredictable weather! Some of my guests have been delayed, but others will arrive at any moment, at which point I must be a proper host. Please, show what you intend to show, without delay."

Calvin and Jonathan exchanged glances. So much for their grand presentation. They now held half the duke's attention, if that.

He took a deep breath. They would make it work.

"Have you seen ladies' fashion repositories such as Ackermann's and La Belle Assemblée?" He motioned for Jonathan to hand over the stack of illustrations. There was no time to select specific favorites. "The Fit for a Duke catalogue will comprise illustrations such as these, organized by type and style, with a clear price for each and information on how to place an order."

A frown marred the duke's regal brow. "Who painted these?"

"Er..." Calvin's poise deserted him along with the rest of his carefully planned speech.

"Mrs. Lépine," Jonathan answered brightly. "A temporary assistant."

The duke snorted softly. "I once had a hedgehog named Lépine."

Calvin closed his eyes. Belle had taken her pseudonym after her brother's childhood pet?

Quickly, he moved to the manikin and began to point out various aspects of its carefully detailed attire. "Here, we can see—"

A distant door blew open and footsteps rushed down the corridor.

Belle burst into the parlor without removing her hat or gloves or the snow clinging to her hair and shoulders.

His chest lightened at the sight of her—he could not help himself—followed by an immediate sickening dip in his stomach. Her presence would ruin everything, if the duke so much as *suspected*—

"Calvin," she breathed.

"*Belle?*" said the duke in obvious befuddlement. "How the devil do you know—"

"Who on earth is—" Jonathan whispered at the same time.

"Mrs. Lépine," said Belle.

"Oh," Jonathan said. "That explains everything."

"*You're* the hedgehog?" Nottingvale roared, a question that made shockingly more sense than it ought.

"And your sister Lady Isabelle," she assured the duke as though his face weren't the shade of an overripe strawberry. She curtsied to Jonathan. "You must be Mr. MacLean."

Jonathan made a fabulous leg. "At your service."

"Nobody is at her service!" The duke whirled on his sister. "Explain yourself."

"I will. But not to you."

From the dumbfounded expression on Nottingvale's face, this was the first time his sister had defied him. Or perhaps it was the first time his will had ever been thwarted at all.

"Calvin," she said again, once she was standing right before him, close enough to touch. "I treated you poorly. You did not deserve it. I was a fool."

"Belle," warned the duke. "If you do not explain yourself at once..."

She spun toward him. "What shall I explain? That you believe me a silly flibbertigibbet? Or shall I inform you that contrary to my family's beliefs, I have my own thoughts and my own interests and pursuing them is the only time I have ever felt free?"

The duke folded his arms across his broad chest. "Am I to presume one such interest you've pursued is the tailor standing before me?"

Calvin's palms went clammy. There it went. His project, his life, the investment, any business relationship with Jonathan, his financial future, all because he couldn't keep his breeches buttoned.

If Belle would just stop talking, she would at least have a chance of saving herself and her reputation.

"Belle, I haven't the patience for nonsense. You may go to your chamber, and gentlemen, it seems we are finished. I am sorry we did not have time for your presentation, but I am no longer in the market for—"

"Now who's spouting nonsense?" Belle's hazel eyes flashed with anger. "If you dismiss this opportunity out of hand, the biggest fool in the room is *you*."

Nottingvale's shocked expression matched Calvin's and Jonathan's. "What do you know about—"

"I painted the sketches, didn't I? The designs are breathtaking. The catalogue is brilliant. It will quickly be the talk of the town. *Every* town, not just London. These men deserve your respect and your attention. If you are too arrogant to listen, I will invest in your place and cut you out completely."

"I thought we were finished," Jonathan whispered. "And now we're in a... bidding war?"

"Belle," Nottingvale said patiently. "The name of the couture is Fit for a *Duke*."

"And you think your shoulders are the only ones broad enough to support it? The name is Fit for a Duke, not 'Fit for His Arrogance, the Duke of Nottingvale.' I know all the same dukes you do, two of which spend their Yuletide here in Cressmouth. I could find a willing replacement by walking down the street."

"You... would never," the duke sputtered.

"Are you so insightful about others?" Belle asked. "Then you must have realized Calvin is just as talented at designing fashions for women as for men. I could help him start an even bigger empire by expanding in that direction. Just watch."

Belle tossed her hat and gloves onto a wing chair. She shrugged out of her pelisse and flung it atop in an unceremonious heap.

She was wearing the gown Calvin had designed for her.

His chest tilted. She did not *need* to wear it. Now that her maid was healthy, Belle could wear any gown in her collection without need of Calvin's hands or his designs. She'd chosen to wear it anyway. She thought it brilliant.

He stared at her in wonder. As big as he and Jonathan had thought they were thinking, Belle was already past them, thinking even bigger. She didn't just believe in him. She was confident enough to put her reputation behind it.

"Walk away if you like," she said to her brother. "It would be a mistake. One I shan't be repeating. Anyone with half a brain can recognize a treasure worth keeping."

She took a deep breath and turned to Calvin.

"I have spent the last four-and-twenty years trying so hard to live up to everyone else's idea of what I should be, that I never had time to fathom out what *I* wanted." Her eyes held his. "Now I know."

His chest pounded uncomfortably loud. He could not look away.

"I love you," she said simply. "The life I want is one with you, whatever it might be. I know you think you spent the past fortnight with a chimera—"

"He *what?*" the duke exploded.

"Excellent reason to be late to the meeting," Jonathan whispered.

Calvin ignored both of them.

"I have never been more myself than in the moments I shared with you." Her eyes glistened. "You weren't wasting your time with a mirage. I'm a real woman, with a few false names. The rest of my life received a false front, but what I had with you was real. I don't want to lose that, and I don't want to lose you."

He still loved her, of course. And he believed that she had enjoyed their time together just as much as he did. But her objections to the match were based on facts that had not changed.

"You're a lady," he pointed out. "I'm a common tailor."

"An *un*common tailor." Her eyes twinkled. "With many fine talents that shall not be named in polite company."

The Duke of Nottingvale groaned into his palms.

"I don't fit in your social circles," Calvin pointed out. "If you marry me, neither will you."

"I don't enjoy the beau monde," she assured him. "Have you met my brother? He's positively insufferable."

Calvin used to believe everyone in the haut ton must be awful. He never thought he'd be able to withstand a single moment in the company of his "betters."

But then he'd met Belle, and experienced the best fortnight of his life with a woman who was secretly the sister of a duke. She wasn't some nameless, faceless aristocrat, but rather a talented, flawed, vulnerable, multifaceted person, just like anyone else.

Except he couldn't make do with just anyone else. He'd fallen for Belle.

He took her hands in his.

"I want you no matter what your name is. I loved you when you were Mrs. Lépine, I loved you when you were Belle, and I still love you even when you're Lady Isabelle."

"You say that like it's bad." The duke harrumphed. "I, for one, honor and respect my title and my position, and will wed as befits my station."

"Five quid says Fate has other plans," Jonathan whispered.

"Make it twenty," Belle whispered back. "The high and mighty are difficult to topple."

"I can *hear* you," the duke ground out.

Belle squeezed Calvin's hands, her eyes bright with mischief and love. "There's only one thing I want. And it's you."

"There had better be two things," he warned her. "Your picture book will make just as big a splash as Fit for a Duke. And it shall have *your* name on it." He grinned at her. "I cannot wait to be known as Mrs. McAlistair's husband, Calvin."

She grinned back at him. "And I cannot wait to be known as Mr. McAlistair's wife, Belle."

"I suppose you lot want my blessing," Nottingvale drawled.

"We don't need it," Belle informed him. "I'm past the age of majority."

"Well, you have it anyway," the duke grumbled. "You're my sister. Of course I want you to be happy. Mother's reaction, on the other hand..."

"Pah." Belle's eyes sparkled. "Mother is too proper to question the word of a duke. She'll be forced to make merry by her own rules. Oh!" She glanced over Calvin's shoulder at Jonathan. "Calvin told me how clever you are with accoutrements to complement each wardrobe. You should meet my friend Angelica Parker. She's a brilliant jeweler."

Jonathan cleared his throat. "I may have... already met her."

*B*elle curled her fingers about Calvin's arm. Her brother's party was underway, and it was nothing less than a spectacular crush.

The first ball was always open to everyone. Guests had arrived from all corners of England, and plenty more had walked or taken a sleigh ride over from Marlowe Castle or the nearby cottages.

Calvin was nervous among so many strangers, so Belle had made it her mission to ensure all the familiar faces did not remain strangers to him for long. It was thrilling to introduce Calvin as her betrothed. Who would have thought that one day Belle would overshadow her important brother at his own party?

But more importantly, she wanted Calvin to feel at ease and at home, so he could come to love Cressmouth just as much as she did. As for him becoming beloved in return, he was well on his way. Vale had dozens of the Fit for a Duke illustrations hung up about the ballroom, and everyone wanted to speak to the visionary who had designed them... and hint that they wouldn't mind their names being at the top of the list when the first catalogue was ready for orders.

"Congratulations, you two lovebirds!"

Belle turned toward the cheery felicitations with a smile. "Calvin, this is my good friend Eve le Duc. She runs the Cressmouth Gazette, a broadsheet delivered monthly to aficionados of our Christmas village all over the country. Eve, this dashing gentleman is the subject of your next front-page column. You won't want to miss your chance to have an exclusive interview with up-and-coming fashion designer and reclusive genius Calvin McAlistair."

"I would love to." Eve had always had ambition, but her eyes positively shone at the idea of publishing an exclusive interview before the big London broadsheets got wind of it. "My office is in the castle. You can drop by or send a note round, and I'll come here. If I arrange a few things..." She tilted her head in thought. "Yes! You'll be in the January issue."

"I hope you'll be mentioning my betrothed as well," Calvin said gruffly, giving Belle's hand on his arm a little squeeze. "I am no lone genius, but rather part of an equally matched team. Belle is an integral part. She not only painted all the illustrations in this room, she also innovated clever ways of promoting Fit for a Duke."

"I'm not the genius he makes me out to be," Belle said, but her cheeks flushed with warmth all the same. "Eve, tell me. What is the primary reason a man who is not a dandy would spend comparable attention to his toilette?"

Eve didn't even need to think it over.

"To attract winsome ladies," she said with a laugh. "Am I right?"

"Of course you're right." Belle grinned back at her. "I'm painting a series of 'before' and 'after' sketches, in which our dear sir is all alone in unimaginative duds, and then becomes the life of the party once he's clothed in attire fit for a duke."

Eve's eyes sparkled. "If you can provide a simple woodcut by Thursday, I'll run it in the January paper. It's always the most popular because everyone wants to see what they missed over Christmas."

Belle nodded. "I'll see that you have it."

"In fact," Calvin added, "we'll be releasing a collector's edition compilation of Belle's illustrations sometime this spring." He gazed at her with pride. "Two books in one year!"

"Two?" Eve repeated in surprise. "What is the first book?"

"Watercolors of life here in Cressmouth," Belle admitted, with a glance up at Calvin beneath her lashes. "I've been painting such scenes for years, but never had the courage to see them published until now. It's not certain yet, of course. We haven't spoken to any publishers."

"It's certain," Calvin said firmly. "They will fight amongst themselves to be the chosen publisher."

"I have no doubt," Eve agreed, then winced.

He frowned. "What is it?"

"Oh, I just saw my husband talking to Belle's brother and realized I hadn't paid my respects yet. If you'll excuse me for a quick moment—"

"Wait," Belle stammered. "Did you just call His Grace... 'Belle's brother?'"

"Well, of course." Eve stared at her quizzically. "That's who he is. Oh, to be sure, he's also now the Duke of Nottingvale et cetera, et cetera. But like most everyone in this village, I've known the two of you since we were small. Belle, and Belle's brother. Easy to remember."

And with that, Eve was gone.

Belle stared up at Calvin. "Did you hear that?"

The corners of his lips quirked as he valiantly tried to hide a smile. "I did. Would you care to explain again who has been living their life in whose shadow? I suppose it's too late to rename the company 'Fit for Belle's brother.'"

She burst out laughing. "Don't tempt me. That sort of mischief is what sisters are for."

He affected an innocent expression. "And what are wives for, may I inquire?"

"I'd rather show you," she answered wickedly. "I hope your dance card is empty. This ballroom is too crowded to spy one's hand in front of one's face. No one will notice if we go missing for a set or two."

"Or three... or four..." His eyes filled with heat and love.

They never did return to the ballroom.

～

# THANK YOU FOR READING

**Love talking books with fellow readers?**

Join the *Historical Romance Book Club* for prizes, books, and live chats with your favorite romance authors:

Facebook.com/groups/HistRomBookClub

And check out the official website for sneak peeks and more:

www.EricaRidley.com/books

# ONE NIGHT WITH A DUKE

12 DUKES OF CHRISTMAS #10

*S*parks fly in this definitely-not-falling-in-love workplace romance between a handsome drifter chasing adventure, and a small-town jeweler who would never leave her home behind...

Dashing Scot Jonathan MacLean never returns to the same town twice. The happy-go-lucky philanthropist seeks constant adventure... and is desperate to outrun his past. When a blizzard traps him in a tiny mountaintop village, he meets a woman who tempts him with dreams he'd long since abandoned: Home. Community. Love. But other people's livelihoods depend on him leaving for good as soon as the snow melts.

Talented jeweler Angelica Parker has spent her life fighting for recognition. She's Black, she's a woman, and she will prove her creations are the equal to any artisan in England. With a contract anchoring her in place for seven years, she lands the project of a lifetime. There's no room for error —or distractions. Such as the charming drifter whose warm embrace and melting kisses have become more precious than jewels...

～

# THE DUKE HEIST

## WILD WYNCHESTERS #1

**A secret identities, forbidden love, opposites attract romance from a *New York Times* bestselling author: Why seduce a duke the normal way, when you can accidentally kidnap one in an elaborately planned heist?**

Chloe Wynchester is completely forgettable -- a curse that gives her the ability to blend into any crowd. When the only father she's ever known makes a dying wish for his adopted family of orphans to recover a missing painting, she's the first one her siblings turn to for stealing it back. No one expects that in doing so, she'll also abduct a handsome duke.

Lawrence Gosling, the Duke of Faircliffe, is tortured by his father's mistakes. To repair his estate's ruined reputation, he must wed a highborn heiress. Yet when he finds himself in a carriage being driven hell-for-leather down the cobblestone streets of London by a beautiful woman who refuses to heed his commands, he fears his heart is hers. But how can he sacrifice his family's legacy to follow true love?

"Erica Ridley is a delight!"
—Julia Quinn

"Irresistible romance and a family of delightful scoundrels... I want to be a Wynchester!"
—Eloisa James

～

# ACKNOWLEDGMENTS

As always, I could not have written this book without the invaluable support of my critique partner, beta readers, and editors. Huge thanks go out to Erica Monroe and Tessa Shapcott. You are the best!

Lastly, I want to thank the *12 Dukes of Christmas* facebook group, my *Historical Romance Book Club,* and my fabulous street team. Your enthusiasm makes the romance happen.

Thank you so much!

# ABOUT THE AUTHOR

Erica Ridley is a *New York Times* and *USA Today* best-selling author of witty, feel-good historical romance novels, including the upcoming THE DUKE HEIST, featuring the Wild Wynchesters. Why seduce a duke the normal way, when you can accidentally kidnap one in an elaborately planned heist?

In the *12 Dukes of Christmas* series, enjoy witty, heartwarming Regency romps nestled in a picturesque snow-covered village. After all, nothing heats up a winter night quite like finding oneself in the arms of a duke!

Two popular series, the *Dukes of War* and *Rogues to Riches*, feature roguish peers and dashing war heroes who find love amongst the splendor and madness of Regency England.

When not reading or writing romances, Erica can be found riding camels in Africa, zip-lining through rainforests in Central America, or getting hopelessly lost in the middle of Budapest.

～

*Let's be friends! Find Erica on:*
www.EricaRidley.com